"How dare you deny you kissed me!"

"I do not deny I kissed you. I merely deny it was meant as a kiss."

"What was your intention, sir?"

"To shock your sister. To make it plain to her that I am a rogue and a villain and not to be thought of in the light of a husband. To send her into such a frenzy that she would die sooner than trust me with her heart."

"I see. You kissed me for my sister's sake."

"Say rather for the sake of the promise I made to discourage your sister's pursuit."

"I am vastly relieved to hear it, my lord, for, in all truthfulness, I mistook it for a kiss."

"Well, I'm dashed to think you mistook me so. If I had meant to kiss you, Miss Cassandra, it would have felt like this."

D1151196

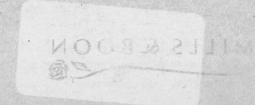

MASK OF
WHITE SATIN

Barbara Neil

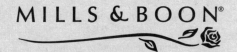

MILLS & BOON®

*All the characters in this book have no existence outside the imagination
of the author, and have no relation whatsoever to anyone bearing the
same name or names. They are not even distantly inspired by any
individual known or unknown to the author, and all the incidents are
pure invention.*

*First published in Great Britain 2001
Harlequin Mills & Boon Limited,
Eton House, 18-24 Paradise Road, Richmond, Surrey TW9 1SR*

© Barbara Sherrod 1992

ISBN 0 263 82727 5

*Set in Times Roman 10½ on 13 pt.
04-0401-60053*

*Printed and bound in Spain
by Litografia Rosés S.A., Barcelona*

Chapter One

Thrown in the Ditch

In all of her one-and-twenty years, Cassandra Vickery had never set eyes on a sea boiling with monstrous green waves, nor a sailing ship foundering on sabre-toothed rocks, nor an outsize pectin shell in the middle of the ocean with a pink-winged sea nymph perched on top. Nevertheless, her water-colours depicted these fantastic images on a pasteboard, one of more than fifty such pasteboards that contained the outpourings of her vibrant imagination.

None of her acquaintance would have suspected that the rector's daughter harboured such colourful fancies beneath her chestnut curls. She invariably gave the appearance of being a sedate, even prim young lady and was generally thought to be the only quiet child of the nine borne by Mrs. Vickery.

It would have shocked her family and neighbours to learn that Miss Cassandra hid an imagination which had ever yearned to burst the confines of Hopcross, one of the smallest and quite possibly one of the dullest villages in England.

If she had lifted her head, Cassandra would have seen in the distance a serene mill pond gleaming in the afternoon sunshine, reflecting an old red-brick mill in all its plain solidity. However, she had known the mill and its pond from girlhood and had long ceased to find them interesting. As she sat on a patch of grass, surrounded by the implements of her art and the bonnet she had taken off so that she might feel the sun on her hair, she kept her eyes steadily on her painting, wholly engrossed in the adventure she had created for her winged heroine. This singular creature wore a diaphanous gown of blue that revealed a quantity of pink skin and a pink ribbon that wound about her waist and neck and interwove with her flowing tresses. Marietta—for that was the sea nymph's name—was on the point of flying from the safety of her shell to rescue the tempest-tossed sailing ship which had foundered and threatened to sink. Because she was not merely a beautiful sea nymph but a fearless one, as well, Marietta had conceived a bold plan. She would swoop down and revive the ship's captain, who lay close to dying. He was a handsome fellow with a dark expression, clipped beard and imperious voice. As soon as he caught sight of the luminous creature who was to save his life and the lives of his salty crew, the dark captain would fall violently in love with her and be transformed by Marietta's goodness into the gentlest of men, though not so gentle as to be tiresome.

"Cassie!" A female voice pierced the charm of her fanciful world. "Cassie, Mama sent me to find you out!"

Instantly, Cassandra secreted the pasteboard beneath an innocuous sheet of sketch paper. The wet paint would certainly smudge, but she had no thought to spare for a little smudging. It was essential to keep her sea nymph well hidden from prying eyes, and most especially from those of her sister, Julia, who was sure to laugh at them unmercifully and expose Cassandra's secret imaginings to the world. More than anything, Cassandra dreaded being thought ridiculous.

"They are coming!" Julia shouted breathlessly as she ran to her sister. "Mama says the news is that they are to arrive at any moment."

Methodically, Cassandra wiped her brush with a cloth, then placed it in its box alongside its fellows. "Who is coming?" she enquired mildly.

Julia paused in her excitement to exclaim, "What do you mean, 'Who is coming'! You know perfectly well who is coming."

"Then I'm afraid I've forgotten."

Julia eyed her sister. "You are an astonishing creature. How can you sit there, fiddling with your paints and nonsense as though I had not just brought you the juiciest titbit you'd ever heard?"

With a narrow red ribbon, Cassandra secured her stack of pasteboards and sketches. "If you will tell me who is coming, I shall do what I may to answer more satisfactorily."

Exasperated, Julia cried, "Whose name has been on everybody's lips? Whom do we speak of every moment, hoping we may catch a glimpse of them?"

"Oh, dear, I am not very clever at riddles. You had best tell me stright out."

"Why, Lord Marcheek, of course. And his cousin, Mr. Bradford."

Cassandra received this triumphant announcement with a blank look.

"Lord Marcheek—heir to the Marquess of Cantywell, and Mr. Bradford, heir to a baronetcy."

"I know who the gentlemen are. If I appear silent, it is because I am at a loss as to what to say."

"Why, say you are delighted, as I am, as Mama is, as we all are."

"Of course I am happy to hear that the marquess may expect a visit from his relations. He has been so kind to our family, to all the families surrounding Cantywell, that I must wish him well, and this attention from his nephews is long overdue.'' She began to gather her implements.

''That is the most tepid reply I have ever heard. Everybody else is in raptures. Mama has never had such excellent gossip to broadcast in the village and has gone to Hopcross on purpose to tell everybody, even though she had just come from there when she heard the news.''

''How did Mama come to hear of it?''

''On her return from Hopcross this morning, she stopped at Cantywell to bring the old marquess a basket of strawberries. He told Mama that he had received a very fine letter from Mr. Bradford, written in a firm and even hand, projecting a visit very soon. Then he showed a portion of the letter to Mama. She saw it with her own eyes. Cantywell is in an uproar making preparations, Mama said.''

''I hope they will not be put to the bother for nothing.''

''I declare, Cassie, this news quite takes my breath away—I could scarcely speak for a full minute when I heard. But while everyone else is beside themselves, you think of nothing but your foolish little paintbox and water-colours.''

''I am sorry to disappoint you, but I cannot expend my poor store of raptures on a pair of gentlemen who have regularly promised to visit their uncle and then have broken their promise with equal constancy. If report is true, Lord Marcheek

is too occupied with flirting in Town to tear himself away.''

''Oh, but this time they really do mean to come.
In his letter, Mama told me, Mr. Bradford said very
particularly that during their stay, he and Lord
Marcheek intended to spend liberally in the village
shops and dance with all the young ladies. That is
proof they mean to come.''

''I hope they will come, Julia, for you and
Mama want them to so very much. But I fear, judging by their past unsteadiness, that they may
change their minds again.'' With an armful of the
accoutrements of her art, she stood and prepared
to accompany her sister along the road to Pilkingdown Rectory.

They walked slowly, for Julia had not done
rhapsodizing and projecting what future joys Lord
Marcheek and Mr. Bradford would bring. The
coming of visitors was such a rarity in the neighbourhood that even were they ugly, mute, aged,
cross and lame, they must excite prodigious interest. The sisters passed a pretty wattle-roofed cot-
tage, where they took a brief short cut through
Dogwood Lane, and emerged onto the highway.
The hedges along the way teemed with leaves of
early summer.

''Mama says that now they are certainly coming,
I am to have a new dress,'' Julia said. ''I hope
Lord Marcheek will like it.''

"You might wear sackcloth and he must like it, for you are by far the prettiest girl he will have the pleasure of seeing during his sojourn in our midst, and if he does not see that at once, then he is a dolt and not worth the expense of the cloth and the trim."

Julia exulted at this compliment. Although the entire county agreed that Miss Julia Vickery's face and figure were so lovely as to cast all other young ladies in the shade, she never tired of hearing herself praised. That the praise should come from a sister who had the irksome habit of never saying anything but what she believed to be true must make it all the more delicious.

"You are too good," Julia said with a brave attempt at modesty, "but Mama will not mind the expense of a new gown, for if his lordship likes it then he may like me in it, and it may be that he will like me very much, and if he should, I should not object to being a marchioness."

Cassandra regarded her sister with concern. "You cannot seriously entertain such hopes, Julia. You are joking. Tell me you are joking."

Offended, Julia enquired, "And why should I joke? Has it never happened that a gentleman born to great position has lost his heart to a young lady of humbler origins? Has it never happened that the son of a gentleman has married the daughter of another gentleman, though the former was blessed with fortune and title and the latter only with respectability and a modest dowry?''

''I have heard of it—in fairy tales.''

Julia snapped, ''Your defect, Cassie, is that you cannot see beyond the nose on your face. You are too practical. I do not know why I spend my time unlocking to you the tender secrets of my heart.''

''I merely wish to prevent your being disappointed.''

''No, you wish to prevent my being happy. You are too dull yourself to understand a creature of my exquisite sensibility.''

Even if Cassandra had known how to dispute this charge, she would not have been allowed to, for a sudden rumble of coach wheels drowned all conversation. Before she was aware, the rushing of horses and the pounding of their hooves on the road kicked up a sudden dusty wind that sent them scrambling to the side of the ditch. While Julia tumbled onto the grass, screaming that she had broken her ankle, Cassandra fell to her knees and watched in despair as her pasteboards flew every which way into the air and came to rest in the ditch-water.

In a heat of anguish, she recalled the years of difficulty, perseverance, and exhilaration that had gone into the making of those now-sodden paintings. Tears started in her eyes and, though she had always disdained women who suffered fainting fits, she felt she might now become one of their number.

She was forced to subdue her distress, however. Julia lay on her back howling in pain at the hazy blue sky. At once Cassandra went to her, knelt by her shoulder, loosened the ribbon of her bonnet so that she might breathe deeply and murmured soothing words. She waved the bonnet so as to give her sister air and begged to know if her rib or back had been injured. At the muffled sound of "ankle," she moved to her sister's feet and endeavoured to divine what devastation lay beneath her soiled cotton stockings. These ministrations proved wholly ineffective. Julia shrieked as though she had been run through with a sword, or, more to the point, as though one of her little brothers had put a toad in her bed. Nothing succeeded in abating the howls until another head appeared beside Cassandra's, the head of a raven-haired young gentleman with a ready smile and a casual enquiry. "Dash it, you ain't hurt, are you? I shall be in a fine pickle if you are."

Cassandra thought the answer so obvious that she expected to hear her sister snap the gentleman's head off, but to her surprise the question immediately silenced Julia.

"Here, I shall help you up," the gentleman said. Gently, he eased his arm around Julia's waist, put his free hand at her elbow and assisted her to her feet.

Although Julia appeared so dazed that she could not take her eyes from the young man's face, Cassandra saw that she was sufficiently mistress of herself to simper, bat her lashes and murmur something heart-rending, in which the words "ankle" and "excruciating" were distinguishable.

As Julia gazed into her rescuer's eyes and he gazed back with a gleam, Cassandra began to be aware of her own superfluity. The sensation was confirmed by Julia's saying, with heavy significance, "Oh, poor Cassie. Your paintings are quite ruined. You must go and see to them at once."

Cassandra was torn between leaving her sister in the arms of a stranger and salvaging what she could from the ditch. She hesitated until Julia whispered irritably, "If you do not go and get your paintings, I shall never forgive you."

Reluctantly, Cassandra turned to the ditch. The sight that greeted her there threw her into an agony of shame, for in the water, nearly up to his boot tops, stood a tall, dark-haired gentleman who bent from time to time, plucked one of her sea-nymph creations from the ditch, and tossed it onto the grass. Because his back was to the sun, which transformed him into a graceful silhouette, she could not make out his features.

She ran to the edge of the ditch and called to

him to stop. He looked at her but she could still not see his face, which was obscured by the shadow of his hat. "Please, do not put yourself to the bother," she cried, wondering what he had seen, wondering if it was too late to prevent his seeing more, wondering if he thought her and her painting romantical and foolish.

"It's the least I can do," he said in a lazy, pleasant tone, "though once my valet sets eyes on these boots, he will no doubt inform me of his intention to seek more respectable employ."

"For your valet's sake, then, I wish you would trouble yourself no further." Out of breath, she knelt by the rescued pasteboards to sift through them as best she could. The colours had run and faded. Vague streaks of blue, yellow and pink dotted the board. No trace remained of a sea nymph in gossamer and ribbons.

"Perhaps my valet will not give his notice," the gentleman said from high above her. "Perhaps he will merely cut me dead for a week. The fellow takes offence when I fall below his high standards."

She saw his wet boots a few inches from her eyes. Looking up, she saw the well-formed face of a gentleman of thirty-four or -five years of age who was regarding her with amusement. A strong suspicion overtook her that he was laughing at her.

"I'm afraid your pictures are quite spoiled," he

said. He placed another three pasteboards on the grass and made as if to return to the water.

Cassandra rose and grasped his sleeve. "Please," she implored, "the paintings cannot be saved. We must forget them and attend to my sister."

He glanced in Julia's direction. The young gentleman held her steady with two strong arms and had her giggling now as loudly as she had howled earlier.

"It appears your sister is quite recovered," the stranger said to Cassandra, and moved again to the water.

Again, Cassandra stopped him. "I assure you, it does not matter about the paintings."

Seriously, he studied her face. "Yes, I can see it does not matter." On that, he waded into the ditch-water, where he pursued two stray pasteboards and brought them to dry land.

Mortified, Cassandra took them from him. "I wish you had not wasted your gallantry on these pasteboards," she said. "Now you will always remember me as the troublesome creature who cost you your valet."

"Never fear. That is not at all how I shall remember you."

Quickly, she glanced at his eyes. If he was laughing at her, she would know the reason why. But his meaning was impossible to read. Judging by his bland expression, he had seen nothing that might make her ashamed of having allowed her fancy to wander at will in water-colour.

"Besides, my cousin and I were entirely at fault here. If he had not decided to take the reins from the coachman and put the chestnuts through their paces, you and your pretty pictures would be well on your way home, or wherever it is that you are headed."

"Oh, you think my pictures are pretty?" she blurted out. "Then you have seen them!"

He paused. "If I say that your pictures are pretty, it is only because the pictures young ladies paint are always pretty. They either show prodigious taste or astonishing skill, never both at once, for that would betoken talent. A young lady must be accomplished, but never talented. Talent represents an excess, and anything in excess is an affront to refined Society."

His calm irony reassured Cassandra for the moment. Thus, she offered no objection when he summoned his servant to gather the paintbox and pasteboards. After the footman had collected them all, the gentleman said, "If your sister is not well enough to walk, our carriage shall certainly be at her disposal."

Together they looked at Julia and her rescuer. The former seemed well enough for dancing in the streets while the latter favoured her with an undisguised leer.

Alarmed for her sister, Cassandra thanked the gentleman for the offer of the carriage and declined.

"If you must walk," he said, "then at least allow my servant to carry your paintings and supplies. You will stain your spencer if you attempt to carry them yourself."

Once more, Cassandra searched his face for evidence of secret knowledge. When she saw a somewhat ironic but amiable smile, she nodded and accepted gladly.

Before the ladies set off, the two gentlemen extended their sincere apologies and bowed. The sisters walked for some time in awed silence, thinking of their late adventure and the elegant, fashionably dressed, gallant gentlemen who had occasioned it. From time to time, Cassandra looked over her shoulder at the stately servant who followed. He carrried the wreckage of her imaginative outpourings as though he were carrying the tea tray at Windsor.

"I am quite certain that was his lordship who saved me," Julia whispered.

"Do you mean Lord Marcheek?"

"Think about it, Cassie. Did you see the crest on the carriage? The coat he wore? The livery of the footmen? They all bespeak a man of fashion, a man of noble blood.''

''They bespeak a man who ought to know better than to race his horses along a narrow highway.''

''I shall ask the servant the name of his master. Then we shall know for certain.''

''I wish you would not. If the gentleman is indeed Lord Marcheek and you do wish him to think well of you, then do not stoop to interrogating his servants.''

''You are right, I suppose. Nothing disgusts a gentleman so much as hearing that a lady has engaged in conversation with her inferiors.''

''That is not at all what I meant, Julia.''

''I suppose the gentleman with his lordship was Mr. Bradford.''

''The tall gentleman who assisted me with my pictures? I suppose he could very well be Mr. Bradford.''

''The gentlemen are equally tall,'' Julia said, as though miffed.

''Were they? Well, then, I should have said the broad-shouldered gentleman.''

''I assure you, Lord Marcheek is every bit as broad-shouldered as his cousin.''

''Now you mention it, he is. It is only that the gentleman who waded in the ditch on my behalf seemed so imposing.''

''That is because he has a forbidding smile

which gives him a disapproving air. I am sure he was looking at me with disapproval. Apart from that, however, the two gentlemen are extraordinarily similar in appearance, which proves that they must be cousins, and no other cousins than Lord Marcheek and Mr. Bradford.''

Cassandra recollected the smile of the gentleman who had assisted her and thought that he might have disapproved of her, as well.

''Still, for all his disapproval, he was excessively kind,'' Julia remarked. ''He ruined his boots merely on account of your silly paintings.''

''Yes,'' Cassandra agreed with a sigh, ''but it was a kindness that it would have been kinder to omit.''

As they drew to the top of a rise, the rectory appeared a little way off the road. It was surrounded by a stone fence adorned with a wildness of vines and shrubs. The path to the house was lined with elms and led to a latticed porch covered with honeysuckle. Cassandra and Julia stopped just outside the door.

''I shall tell Mama that we have met them. It will please her beyond anything to know that her daughters saw them before anyone else.''

Ordinarily, Cassandra would have responded with a caution, saying that they must not make such a claim until they knew for certain the identity of the two gentlemen, but her mind was preoccupied. It had occurred to her that if the gentlemen were in truth Lord Marcheek and Mr. Bradford, then this day's encounter would prove only the first of many meetings. She would be obliged to endure Mr. Bradford's company in future, and she would never see him without blushing for her wildly fanciful pictures and wondering how much he had seen and, worse, how much he had guessed.

Chapter Two

An Uncommon Daisy

Mr. James Bradford, a gentleman of moderate temper and immoderate fortune, refused to enter the carriage until his cousin had agreed to relinquish the reins to the coachman.

"You may be a complete hand in the boudoir, Marcheek," he said, "but you fall far short in the box."

Not offended in the least, his lordship climbed into the carriage. He settled back with as much satisfaction as if he had just proved his superiority with the whip. "Dash it all, James, I do believe I am actually looking forward to seeing our uncle. I had always dreaded such a visit, thinking it must be as tedious as playing a hand without betting on it, but now it strikes me that there are vastly amusing folk in the country."

"You are not here to amuse yourself, cousin," Mr. Bradford said. "You are here because you amused yourself too thoroughly in London and must lie low until the noise abates."

"I only meant that I should have visited Cantywell sooner if I'd known how bracing the air was, how charming the hills and dales, how delightful the rustics."

"How pretty the maidens, you mean," Mr. Bradford replied. "You have been in Hampshire less than two minutes and have already fallen in love."

Sighing, Marcheek said, "I wish I knew her name."

"You might have waited a bit, you know. You might have given me a day's respite from pulling you out of scrapes."

"You wrong me, James. I have no intention of falling into a scrape."

"Your intentions scarcely matter. You have met a pretty, silly coquette and I know what follows next."

"I'm dashed if I even noticed that she was pretty!" Marcheek protested. "My only thought was to rescue two damsels in distress."

"You did not rescue them, if you please. You were the *cause* of their needing to be rescued."

"Were we, indeed? I'd no idea."

"Not *we*. *You* were the one. You nearly ran them and us into the ditch with your recklessness."

"I suppose my uncle will hear of it and hand me a lecture."

"You might redeem yourself, you know," Mr. Bradford suggested. "You might question the servant who escorted the young ladies home. You might find out where he took them and whether he learned their names. If so, then we might pay a visit to them—to enquire after their health."

"That is a capital notion. I should like to see the young lady again, purely to ask after her ankle, you understand."

"Before you place too many hopes on that ankle, you had better make up your mind to behave during the visit, as I expect her family will be about, looking us over and no doubt disliking what they see."

"Dash it, that's coming it a bit strong. No family ever disliked me," Marcheek asserted, "at least no mother did, at least not at first."

"No mother wishes to hear that her daughter's new acquaintance was formed by the circumstance of his nearly trampling her with his horses."

"Ah, I see what you mean." He grew glum. "I suppose we shall all sit in a small, airless country parlour, while the papa growls at me and the mama watches over her girls like a sheepdog protecting her lambs from the hawk. On consideration, James,

I do not care to enquire after the young lady's ankle. You may go yourself and extend my regrets.''

"You are mistaken, Marcheek. There is nothing that would give you more pleasure than to visit the young ladies.''

"There ain't?''

"In fact, you are perishing to pay the visit, so much so that you mean to pay it tomorrow.''

"Tomorrow? I shall scarcely have time to adjust myself to the country climate.''

"You are young. You will bear up.''

"Be so good as to tell me why I am so anxious to make this dashed visit.''

"Because if you do not," Mr. Bradford said pleasantly, "I shall write to Sir Walter and Lady Loveless to inform them of your whereabouts. He will hotfoot it to Hampshire, the better to put a bullet through your rascally skull, and his lady will come to weep over your pitiful but smartly attired corpse. Does that answer your question?''

His lordship sulked. "Perfectly.''

Mr. Bradford waited to be asked why he was so determined that they should pay such an unpromising visit. Indeed, he quite looked forward to being asked, for he was prepared with an excellent excuse—that he wished to study the manners and habits of the locals. Lord Marcheek would believe such an excuse because everyone knew Mr. James Bradford to be a man of wide curiosity, a gentleman who had travelled to the Indies, the Orient, even to the Americas, in search of the rarest, the most beautiful, the most wondrous of sights. But Marcheek was too engrossed in his own concerns to ask, and so Mr. Bradford had no opportunity to disguise his real motive, which had taken firm root the instant he had seen a painting of a stormy sea and sky and in the midst of it, a delicate, enchanting sea nymph.

The painting had been attached to a piece of sketch paper containing a pencil drawing of an unexceptionable daisy. When he had removed the sketch, he had found the pasteboard underneath. Astounded at what he saw, he would have enjoyed looking at it for a considerable time, except that the artist herself had called out to him then, begging him to leave the paintings to drown. He had been obliged to replace the daisy sketch and deliver up the treasure.

He would have complimented the young lady on her skill and originality, but it had been instantly clear that she was mortified beyond speech. Fear enlarged her blue eyes, so that he had refrained from telling her that he had not only seen her picture but he wished to see others. She had been greatly relieved when he had pretended not to have seen anything. Subsequently, he had endeavoured to speak only on indifferent matters, to put her mind at ease and to allay any suspicion that he had invaded the most private precincts of her imagination. By assuming the blandest of airs, he had at last succeeded in soothing her.

But having soothed her, he could not soothe himself. He could not get the picture out of his head. Never had he seen anything quite like it anywhere in his travels. He had certainly never expected to encounter anything of the sort in the sleepy villages of Hampshire. The ship seemed fragile against the tumultuous rolling waves, the bulging clouds and the blackened sky; a scene that hinted at a force of emotion in the artist. Unaccountably, in the midst of the composition was a sea nymph, whose clothing consisted of veils that billowed sensuously round her form. The scene was expressive of a wild, romantical imagination. No doubt that was why the artist had been so conscious. No doubt she was aware that in an age of mild, decorous art, she had conceived a seascape replete with extravagant feeling. But if that was the cause of the artist's mortification, it was also the cause of his admiration. What was the nymph doing there, he wanted to know. What did she have to do with the ship? Where had she come from? What would become of her?

It was a picture that those who did not know better might think wicked or silly or mad. He, however, had seen specimens of the wicked, the silly and the mad during his travels and knew precisely what they looked like. They bore no resemblance to the young lady's picture, which was powerful, mysterious and fresh. There was no time to lose, he felt, in meeting again with the artist, for she had given him that rarest of pleasures: a surprise.

The Marquess of Cantywell and his household, from the poorest stablehand to the formidable housekeeper, Mrs. Clapshew, were beside themselves with joy at the arrival of the two gentlemen. Their uncle hobbled out the door without his coat as soon as the wheels of their carriage sounded in the drive. He pumped his nephews' hands, slapped them on their broad shoulders and promised them a multitude of delights and entertainments, beginning with a drink of tea.

"Tea?" groaned Lord Marcheek. "Is that the best you have, Uncle?"

"Ah, you prefer lemonade," cried the old gentleman. "Lemonade it shall be." The housekeeper was bidden to fetch a pitcher of lemonade to the drawing-room.

As they followed their uncle inside, Lord Marcheek whispered to Mr. Bradford, "Take pity on your only cousin, James, and do not let him feed me any dashed lemonade. I cannot defile my innards with such a vile brew."

"I shall inform him that your innards are sensitive to anything but the rankest brandy and gin."

"I am forever in your debt."

During a quarter hour spent in the drawing-room, the uncle itemized the amusements in store for the lads, as he was pleased to call them: rides through the countryside, walks to the village and, especially, visits with the neighbours. Never was an old man so blessed, the marquess declared, as he was in his neighbours. They called every day to see whether he was still alive. They brought him angelica and news from the village. They brought poultices and puddings when he was ill. Who could ask for more?

"I shall ask for more brandy," Lord Marcheek said, helping himself to another glass.

Mr. Bradford took genuine pleasure in his uncle's good-natured prattle and accepted the offer of a pipe, though he did not take snuff or tobacco as a rule.

Yawning, Marcheek asked his uncle where the nearest gaming house might be found. On learning that such a thing did not exist in Hopcross, he said *sotto voce* to his cousin, "Let this serve as a lesson to me—whenever I misbehave in London, I shall soon find myself banished to Hampshire. That knowledge will force me to behave myself."

The marquess, thinking everybody as content as he, smiled and nodded and plied his heir with more brandy.

Mr. Bradford excused himself, found the library

and sent for the servant who had followed the young ladies to Pilkingdown Rectory. The man reported that the young ladies were sisters, that they were the elder daughters of Mr. Vickery, the rector, and that as soon as Mrs. Vickery had assured herself of her girls' safety, she had grown quite faint at the honour accorded them in being nearly killed by two gentlemen of refinement and fashion.

During the report, Mr. Bradford remained serious and silent, but as soon as the servant bowed himself off, he permitted himself to say aloud, "Ah, her name is Cassandra."

The following day, at the hour Mr. Bradford had appointed, he and his cousin set out on their visit.

When Lord Marcheek heard what the servant had said of the two young ladies, he complained, "They not only have parents, but there are seven sisters and brothers. There will be no getting at the two of them."

Mr. Bradford disdained to notice this self-serving view of the visit, but Marcheek's words proved prophetic, for when the gentlemen entered the cheerful, sunny parlour at the rectory, they found the entire family gathered, the younger children snuggled near the feet of the elder, listening to their father read, or rather, declaim, from a large, much-worn Bible.

Overcome by the honour done to her humble

house, Mrs. Vickery could not make the visitors welcome enough, especially as they were both fine-figured, handsome gentlemen. At first, she could not tell which was the heir to the marquess and which was the future baronet, but as they were both eligible, rich and due to inherit a title, she fawned on them equally.

"You are welcome, gentlemen," the rector intoned, and before anything beyond the barest introduction could take place, Mr. Bradford and his lordship were given the best chairs and treated to the story of Noah and his remarkable ark.

The story had a stupefying effect. Though it was the middle of the day and the listeners were all as lively and ruddy as healthy young Englishfolk ought to be, the rector's sonorous voice soon sent several of them into a doze. Those who were unfortunate enough to remain awake, shifted and squirmed and barely suppressed grunts of boredom. Oblivious to his audience's misery, the rector droned on about the number of cubits of gopher-wood required to house every kind of creeping thing on Earth. Mr. Bradford could not help but take pity on them all, on himself most of all. The instant the rector paused for breath, he interjected smoothly, "By a curious coincidence, Mr. Vickery, I have recently come from a tour of Mount Ararat."

Every eye turned on him. He looked from one

curious face to the next until his gaze rested on Cassandra's. It pleased him to see that he had piqued her interest.

"Mercy!" the rector exclaimed in some awe. "You have actually climbed the mountain where Noah's ark came to rest?"

"It was not precisely a mountain. In fact, it could scarcely be called a hill. It was a slight rise in the desert, but my guide assured me it had once been Mount Ararat and he produced a piece of timber which he claimed was a remnant of the ark itself, as well as a snuffbox, which bore the crest of the House of Noah. He offered to sell me the articles at a great bargain, but, as I had already purchased a vial of Flood waters, I was obliged to decline."

"Did you see a camel?" one of the children enquired.

"I *rode* a camel," he replied.

While their father shook his head and mourned the decay of holy sites, and their mother thanked the visitors for honouring her children with such civil answers to their questions, the little ones gathered round the stranger in some awe.

"Did you see an elephant?" one asked.

"I *rode* an elephant," Mr. Bradford replied.

"Did you see a tiger?"

"I hope you did not *ride* a tiger," Cassandra said.

He looked at her and was struck by the laughter in her eyes.

"I did indeed see a tiger," he said. "Happily, I was not asked to ride him. But I did observe an entire family of tigers on the prowl, and very fierce they were, too." Cassandra did not gasp audibly as her younger siblings did, he noted, but she kept her eyes on him intently. "They were magnificent," he added. "They are quiet, graceful, powerful beasts." To his pleasure, Cassandra gazed far off, as though she could imagine a tiger in all its golden splendour.

"My cousin has travelled the world over," Marcheek put in. "I myself find travelling dashed exhausting. I prefer to stay at home, among good friends." He cast a heavy-lidded smile at Julia and received a brilliant one in return.

"Have you indeed seen so many strange places?" Cassandra asked Mr. Bradford. "Have you seen Athens? Have you seen Florence?"

"Yes, indeed. I have also seen Cadiz, Constantinople, Cairo and the purported remains of ancient Carthage. I have even seen New York."

The rector's head snapped up. "Surely, you did not visit New York. We are at war with the Americans."

"We were not at war at the time that I was privileged to visit. When this war is ended, I hope to visit again."

"You do not mean to visit a nation which impresses our sailors!"

"Papa," Cassandra said, "it is we who impress their sailors."

"Oh. Well, if so, I'm certain we do it for very good reason."

Mrs. Vickery bustled the younger children off to the nursery in the charge of their nurse. She then invited Mr. Vickery to retire to the sanctuary of his study, where he might ponder the remainder of Noah's adventures without interruption. These manoeuvres successfully completed, she enquired of the gentlemen whether they would do her daughters the honour of accompanying them on a walk. There was a pretty prospect near Tickleton Farm, she said, and the girls would like nothing better than to show it to them.

"Capital," Marcheek declared. "There is nothing like a heavy dose of Bible to make one long for fresh air and sunshine."

"I should be pleased to see the prospect," Mr. Bradford said, "and perhaps Miss Cassandra may be prevailed on to draw a sketch of the scene for us. I wonder," he continued, looking directly at her, "whether you would be so kind as to bring your sketch paper and pencils. I should be delighted to carry them for you."

Cassandra stiffened. Something in his words and tone aroused the suspicion that he had seen her paintings, glimpsed the fruits of her untamed fancies and guessed at the immoderate sensations that had prompted the creation of such a creature as Marietta. He had done what she feared most—misconstrued her meaning and read into it something lascivious. Nothing, she told herself, not the threat of torture on the rack, would induce her to sketch for him.

But when she glanced at his face, he appeared so bland, so absorbed in returning her mother's compliments, so little attentive to what she might answer that she was forced to dismiss her fears. Besides, she recollected, he had spoken of her sketch paper and pencils rather than her watercolours. If he had seen anything, it was her pencil sketches, not her paintings. She had not been found out, after all.

As soon as she had fetched her bonnet and drawing implements, they set out for Tickleton Farm. Although Julia and Marcheek walked quickly, in hopes of outstripping the other two, Cassandra insisted on keeping pace with them. It gave her no little concern to see her older sister flirting recklessly with a man who bore the reputation of being an outrageous trifler. She could scarcely attend to her companion, so engrossed was she in what might be passing between Julia and Lord Marcheek. With every smile he levelled at her sister, her alarm intensified.

"You are out of breath, Miss Cassandra," Mr. Bradford said. "Perhaps we might walk more slowly."

"There is nothing I like so well as being out of breath," she assured him, hastening even more.

Having failed to elude their companions, Julia and Marcheek changed their tactics. They dawdled until they languished some distance behind the other pair. Cassandra slowed her steps to such a degree that Mr. Bradford observed, "You no longer like being out of breath, I see. Now nothing pleases you as well as a snail's pace."

"The truth is, Mr. Bradford, I do not wish to lose sight of my sister."

Glancing back, Mr. Bradford saw his cousin gazing softly into his companion's eyes. Mr. Bradford scarcely saw Julia; to him she was exactly like the Town girls who set their caps at Marcheek every day. Still, he knew, it would not do to have his cousin seduce one of the village daughters, especially one from a respectable family. The upshot would be that he, James Bradford, would be forced to quit the county to help his cousin escape another scandal, and he had no intention of leaving so soon. He rather fancied Hampshire, fancied Hopcross, fancied the rectory and its residents, especially one of them, and he would be, in the words of his cousin, dashed if he would go before he had learned a great deal more about her.

*   *   *

They attained the edge of a low cliff lined with soft shrubs and wild flowers. In the valley below lay Tickleton Farm. Its main house and buildings gleamed rosily against the rolling green fields. A narrow canal divided the farm from Hopcross Church, with its grey spire reaching high above the landscape. On one side of the canal stood trees dense with leaves and white spraying flowers. On the other, a herd of black-and-white cows stood like statues grazing in the clover. Mr. Bradford marvelled at the peaceful beauty of the scene, while Cassandra marvelled at her sister's imprudence. To her dismay, she observed that Julia was whispering behind her hand to Lord Marcheek.

It was not many minutes before Mr. Bradford grew sensible of his companion's uneasiness and divined the cause. He called to his cousin to join him in watching Miss Cassandra at her sketching. Lord Marcheek sauntered to the spot where they sat, knelt beside Cassandra and assisted her by untying her pencils. When Cassandra looked up, she was relieved to see a sullen Julia join them.

The four gazed at the farm for a time, until Julia gave a great sigh and declared that she wished with all her heart that Papa would take her to London. She would perish with boredom if she did not visit Town. Country life was too narrow and unvaried to satisfy a creature of her sensibility.

Mr. Bradford interrupted to enquire, ''What

shall we ask your sister to draw? The farm, the fields, the church? There are so many attractive subjects to choose from.''

Julia treated him to a look of distaste. "What does it matter what she draws?''

"I think Miss Cassandra ought to draw Tickleton Farm,'' declared Lord Marcheek. "It is a dashed pretty picture already. Therefore, she cannot go far wrong.''

Mr. Bradford urged Cassandra to heed this suggestion. "An artist must be grateful to have such a fine model. You may draw from life as it truly is.''

She regarded him steadily, once again doubting what he knew and did not know. "It may be preferable to draw from imagination,'' she said. "Do you think an artist must always have the model before her eyes?''

"I am not an artist, and so I cannot answer.''

She coloured. "Nor am I. I merely sketch a little.''

"I should like to see one of your sketches.''

Conscious, she looked down. Then glancing hastily about her, she declared, "I believe I shall sketch that daisy.''

They all looked at the edge of the cliff, where a clump of wilted daisies nodded in the sunlight. One of them stood a trifle higher than the others, with its face turned fully forward. "Yes,'' Cassandra

said, "you shall have that daisy," and she proceeded to draw the most clumsy, squat-looking
growth that ever had the effrontery to call itself a
flower.

This daisy, she calculated, would put an end to
any curiosity Mr. Bradford might have concerning
her pictures. She would make him a present of it.
He would be sorry he ever asked her to draw anything at all.

As soon as she set to work on the daisy, Julia
and Marcheek saw their opportunity. Mr. Bradford
peered intently over Cassandra's shoulder and paid
them no more mind than Cassandra did. Therefore,
they were able to steal away, to stroll at will
around a generous hawthorn, and to titter at each
other with conscious looks.

"You do not find the daisy a somewhat prosaic
subject?" Mr. Bradford asked Cassandra.

"Not at all." Her pencil traced the line of an
overly thick stem, out of which grew appendages
which greatly resembled worms. "I have read that
there is as much art in the prosaic as in the exotic,"
she said.

"There is," he agreed, "for the artist who finds
what is true and universal in the prosaic. But the
artist whose imagination flies must look for uncommon subjects."

"Perhaps your wide travels have made you un-
appreciative of the prosaic, Mr. Bradford. Perhaps

you ought to be reminded that there may be prodigious pleasure in what is...what is..."

"Dull?"

"I meant to say *commonplace*."

"There is nothing commonplace in your daisy.
Indeed, I have never seen anything quite like it."

"Then it is yours, Mr. Bradford. You may have
it as a keepsake."

She tore the paper from her sketch-book and
handed it to him.

As he studied it, he smiled, for although it was
hideous, it contained a hint of flowing grace in its
lines. It had humour in the suggestion of a scowl
on the daisy's face. It had delicacy in the form of
the petals. Miss Cassandra had not quite succeeded
in disguising her talent.

"I thank you," he said. "I shall never look at a
daisy in the same way again."

Cassandra allowed suspicions to fade. If Mr.
Bradford knew so little of art as to be grateful for
her sketch, she had nothing to be alarmed about.

No sooner had she decided that she might be
perfectly easy than she spotted Julia with Lord
Marcheek. They held their heads close together, as
though engaged in plotting some mischief. A troubled expression crossed her face, and, observing it,
Mr. Bradford too looked in the direction of the
hawthorn tree. He was on the point of interrupting
the tête-à-tête when Marcheek and Julia came skip-

ping towards them, laughing and demanding their attention.

"I have thought of a scheme," his lordship informed them. "And a dashed delightful one it is, too."

"Mama will be in raptures," Julia said.

His lordship went on: "I propose that my uncle give a ball in my honour. In your honour, too, of course, James, but mostly in mine, because I thought of the plan to begin with."

Cassandra tried to imagine it—a ball. It had been some time since an entertainment had been got up in Hopcross for the purpose of dancing and merriment. A private party had been given in November by one of the squires, but he had not deigned to invite any of the neighbourhood families. For the Marquess of Cantywell to give a ball was a cause for pleasure. She felt her imagination stir at the word.

"I shall lay the notion before my uncle," Marcheek declared, "and he will be happy to oblige. The poor old fellow cannot do enough for us. It will make him the happiest creature alive to go to vast inconvenience for our sake."

Mr. Bradford enquired, "Miss Cassandra, do you approve of the plan? Perhaps a ball is not prosaic enough for your taste."

She glanced down at her hands. "I should very much like to attend a ball."

He enjoyed the sight of her flaming cheeks. "But balls are so dull. I assure you, I have been to thousands, and they are nothing but large crushes in hot, airless rooms. One is unable to move or talk with any measure of comfort."

Marcheek and Julia protested against this unjust representation of balls.

"I have never been to one," Julia cried, "but I am certain they must be the liveliest things."

"Oh, indeed they are," Marcheek assured her, "for the host always brings out his best wine for the occasion and the stakes at the card table are nearly high enough to suit even my taste."

"You may like a ball, Marcheek," Mr. Bradford said, "but Miss Cassandra is so devoted to the commonplace that I'm afraid she may be disappointed."

"Then we must contrive a way to make certain she is not," said Marcheek.

"Oh, do find a way," Julia cried, "for I do not like to be disappointed, either. I always like to have everything exactly as I wish it to be."

Mr. Bradford smiled at the sight of Miss Cassandra's uneasiness. If he provoked her sufficiently, he thought, she might for a moment drop her veneer of primness and reserve.

"Dash it all," Marcheek exclaimed, "what if it were to be a masquerade ball!"

"Oh, yes!" Cassandra exclaimed. Then, blushing fiercely, she was quick to amend her proposal. "Of course, I would not wish to suggest that the marquess undertake anything likely to give rise to talk. Such a thing would surely offend him as well as his neighbours if it were associated with intrigue and licence."

"Cecilia attended a masquerade in the novel by Miss Burney," Julia cried. "Therefore, it cannot be scandalous."

"Romeo and Juliet met at a masquerade," Mr. Bradford said with a smile. Then he added, "However, as I recollect, that meeting did not turn out very well in the end."

"The ball I speak of would not be a masquerade," Cassandra hastened to explain. "It would be a private masked ball. A masquerade might give a very wrong impression, as well as inconvenience those who are unable to devise a costume. We shall have to ask Papa, of course, but I do not think even he will find much that is objectionable in a private masked ball."

"No, indeed!" Marcheek exclaimed. "James and I have lately attended a private ball of that kind, and it was unexceptionable. I'm dashed if I wasn't delighted."

"You fell asleep, if I recall."

Ignoring his cousin, Lord Marcheek stretched out his hand to congratulate Cassandra on her suggestion, and when she extended hers, he shook it heartily. Cassandra smiled shyly at him.

The exchange was not lost on Mr. Bradford, who began to suspect his cousin of flirting with the younger as well as the older of the Vickery daughters. Miss Cassandra was interesting and attractive, lively and intelligent beneath her air of quiet elegance. Her sister, on the other hand, was tiresome and insipid. Even Marcheek, who never looked beyond a pretty face, must grow weary of Miss Julia's. He would have to be a thoroughgoing dunce not to prefer the one sister to the other. And if he did, it would not be the first time he had captured the hearts of two sisters. Indeed, he had once contrived to have three generations of a single family in love with him at the same time. To prevent history's repeating itself, Mr. Bradford determined to keep a close eye on his cousin. If he was flirting with Miss Cassandra, he would soon be made to think better of it. As to Miss Cassandra, if she were capable of being charmed by Marcheek, he would be exceedingly disappointed in her.

The exchange was not lost on Julia, either, and seeing her sister glaring at her, Cassandra quickly pulled her hand away from Marcheek's, saying, "But perhaps the purpose of the ball is to introduce the marquess's nephews to the neighbourhood. In that event, a masked ball would seem to inhibit such an introduction rather than promote it."

At this logic, Marcheek's face fell. Julia pouted. "You are far too practical, Cassie."

"Your sister is practical indeed," said Mr. Bradford. "Unlike the rest of us, she is mindful of such vexatious necessities as reason and sense. She sees something to admire in the commonplace, and takes no pleasure in what is scandalous or offensive. I suppose that, unlike you, Miss Vickery, she has no wish to see London. Therefore, it is no wonder that she prefers a private masked ball to a masquerade."

Incensed at his tweaking tone, Cassandra defended herself. "You make me out a perfect prig, Mr. Bradford, but you mistake me. I should like nothing better in all the world than to see London and to dance at a masquerade. However, I do not believe in pleasing myself at the cost of injuring others. I should regret it profoundly if your uncle were persuaded to do a thing that would cause him no end of mortification. I could have no pleasure in either a journey to Town or a masquerade, however splendid, if it produced such a result."

Mr. Bradford regarded Cassandra in some amusement. He had provoked her as much as he had hoped, and she had proven herself even more spirited and lovely than he had imagined. He saw that though she gave the appearance of being the very opposite of her sister—proper, restrained, dignified—there was, in point of fact, one profound similarity. Both young ladies longed to see what lay beyond the confines of Hopcross. Both looked to experience adventure. It was the combination of the rational and romantical in Cassandra that most excited his interest.

"What is that?" Marcheek demanded. He pointed to the sketch which Cassandra had lately bestowed on Mr. Bradford.

"It is a daisy," said Mr. Bradford. "Miss Cassandra has been so kind as to make me a present of it."

"Dash it, I don't see why you ought to have it, James. You have all those other pictures hanging about, all those Dutch and Italian thingumabobs. I daresay, one would think you meant to live in a museum the way you go about collecting pictures. You might spare one for me, for I do not have a picture to my name, at least not one as pleasant as this daisy. All my pictures portray my ancestors, who, by the look of them, must have suffered the most violent dyspepsia."

Cassandra glanced in alarm at Mr. Bradford. It mortified her to know that she had given the very worst example of her skill to a man who was a collector. At once, she rose and offered, "Mr. Bradford, if you will give Lord Marcheek this daisy, I shall draw you another."

Mr. Bradford also stood. He smiled at her because she avoided his eyes, and to Cassandra's infinite chagrin, he replied, "I would not part with it for the world. It is one of a kind. I will never gaze on it without thinking of the artist and her excess of kindness in giving it to me."

Chapter Three

Secrets

The Marquess of Cantywell was not behindhand in introducing his nephews to his neighbours. He arranged a party which was accounted prodigiously fashionable by the county folk and prodigiously countrified by Lord Marcheek. It provided five card tables, an abundance of white soup and wine and Mrs. Vickery at the harpsichord in the event that the young people might wish to roll back the rug and dance a reel.

By the time the party took place, Lord Marcheek and Mr. Bradford had already improved their acquaintance with the young ladies of the rectory, owing to Miss Julia Vickery's numerous hints to his lordship regarding walks to the village, visits to the chemist's and calls of charity among the farmhouses. On these occasions, the gentlemen fell in with the young ladies' plans, whatever they were, and as Julia and Marcheek always had much to say to each other that excluded all others, Cassandra was invariably left to Mr. Bradford's company. She was intrigued enough by his reputation as a traveller to venture a question now and again about some distant capital, but feared him enough that she was often quiet and withdrawn. To put her at ease, he spoke exclusively on unexceptionable matters. Eventually, he exhausted the topics of the climates, spectacles and customs to be found in every far-flung corner of the globe, and so he, too, was often quiet and withdrawn. At the party, though, he determined that the awkwardness of their recent conversations should be overcome, and accordingly, when he was able to speak with her privately in a corner of the drawing room, he alluded to the subject he knew to be most provoking.

"I have sent your daisy to London for framing," he said.

She stared at him.

Her expression pleased him. At least she had not bowed her head and avoided his eyes as she customarily did. "My task now," he said, "is to decide where to hang it."

"Oh, you do not mean to hang it!"

"Perhaps my London house would provide the most proper setting." He saw her begin to breathe heavily, so that the green ribbon and white lace at her bosom rose and fell rapidly.

"I wish you would not tease me," she said in a low voice, full of emotion.

"Tease you? I mean every word I say, I assure you. Your daisy shall be hung so that I may look at it."

"I am a country girl. I do not understand the manners of the fashionable world. I only know that it is cruel of you to mock me so."

"My dear Miss Cassandra, if you truly believe my intention is to mock, then it is true, as you say, that you do not understand the manners of the fashionable world."

"How can I believe otherwise, when it is manifestly clear, sir, that you are a collector, a connoisseur? You know very well how poor my daisy is. Yet you insist upon praising it beyond its deserts."

"Are you so certain that the praise is undeserved?"

"I am certain that the praise is insincere, which to my mind is mockery, regardless of what you may choose to call it."

Before he could say another word, she walked hastily to where her father sat at cards and pretended to advise him as to the tricks he might take as the play went round.

Mr. Bradford smiled. Miss Cassandra's indignation did her credit in his eyes. As to *her* eyes, which were large and warmly grey, he thought the tears of anger in them enchanting.

These charming reflections were interrupted by Lord Marcheek, who summoned the attention of the company to ask for an opinion as to the desirability of a masked ball at Cantywell.

"A masked ball?" the old marquess said. "I do not recall such a thing ever taking place hereabouts. We are not so daring as you are in Town, as a rule. We content ourselves with card parties and conversation."

"Then it is time there was a masked ball, Uncle," Lord Marcheek replied. "What do you say, Miss Vickery?" He threw Julia a look of particularity, and another at Miss Cassandra.

Julia simpered with all due modesty and declared, "I vow, I do not know what to say. What do you say, Papa?"

Mr. Vickery set down his cards reluctantly, for he was on the point of throwing down an ace, and assuming his most pontifical air, he pondered. He pondered so long that those who waited to hear his judgement began to shift about and yawn. At last he delivered himself of a clerical verdict, to wit, that a masked ball was not so bad as a masquerade in supplying opportunities for lasciviousnes and licence, but it was bad enough.

When his listeners protested, he was moved to

relent so far as to say, "A masked ball might be an innocent diversion and one I should not be averse to attending, if certain stipulations were met."

He was begged to tell the company what these might be.

"Well, for one thing, the musicians must not be too noisy. The fiddles give one the headache. And for another thing, the card tables must be made up early."

"My uncle will be happy to oblige you, Rector," Marcheek stated. "Will you not, Uncle?"

The marquess was framing an answer when Mr. Vickery continued.

"I further stipulate that the masks of each of the guests be made known in advance," he said. "Where there is no question of identity, there will be no incitement to intrigue."

Julia cried out, "What is the use of a masked ball if everyone's identity is known at the outset?"

Marcheek added his cries to hers. "No intrigue! Dash it, where is the fun in that?"

Immovable, Mr. Vickery perused his cards and selected one to discard. "That is my stipulation," he said with finality, so that the young people were compelled to be content.

Mr. Bradford, who thought the notion of Miss Cassandra wearing a mask most interesting, and Miss Cassandra, who thought the notion of a ballroom full of masked ladies and gentlemen most interesting, waited in high anticipation to see what the old marquess would reply. When he boomed, "It shall be done! It shall be as everybody wishes!" Cassandra found her imagination soaring, while Mr. Bradford found he could not take his eyes from her animated face.

Invitations to the ball at Cantywell were delivered late on Wednesday. By dawn on Thursday, the neighbourhood was buzzing. There were those who found reason to take the ball as a compliment to themselves, namely, Miss Julia Vickery. There were those who had high hopes of snaring one of the eligible gentlemen in whose honour the ball was given, namely, Miss Julia Vickery. And there were those who saw in the occasion an opportunity to carry out a bold plan, namely, Miss Julia Vickery, who burst into the pretty attic chamber she shared with her sister and giggled behind her hand.

The ceiling of the room peaked in the centre and sloped at the sides, so that one was forced to stoop in order to look out the casement. A large high bed covered with a patchwork and boasting four carved posts at the corners filled the better part of the chamber. In a corner near the window stood a small writing table, at which Cassandra was seated, busy at work. Although Julia was, as always, too full of her own affairs to notice what her sister was about, Cassandra deftly hid her water-colour under a pencil sketch the instant she heard the squeak of the door. She had been engaged in creating a fresh adventure for Marietta. Instead of rescuing a ship's captain and his valiant crew, she floated on a sea-shell towards a villa, where a party was going forward on the terrace. It was a ball, a masked ball. The tiny figures who danced under the lustrous moon were sumptuously dressed. They wore purple masks, excepting one gentleman of fine bearing. Unfortunately, Cassandra could not make out his features. She sensed that he was attractive, though not handsome in the conventional way; more than a vague impression of his appearance she could not conjure. She had been trying to picture the gentleman's face when Julia interrupted.

"There is such a to-do!" her sister announced. "Papa is in a violent snit, and all on account of the ball."

Cassandra gathered her pasteboards, and after setting them carefully in a small chest, locked it. "I suppose he has changed his mind and does not wish to attend," she said.

As Julia was occupied at the looking-glass, she did not notice her sister's movements. "Papa feels it his duty to attend, he says, so that the young people do not give themselves entirely up to frivolity. He is in a snit because Mama wishes to have a new ball gown made for me."

Although the living of Pilkingdown was ample, Mr. Vickery considered it his duty as the father of nine children to practise economy of the most stringent sort. "I suppose he objects to the expense," Cassandra said.

"He says I have just had a new dress and it is too soon for me to have another. Mama says I must have the gown, for Lord Marcheek has done me the honour of securing my promise for the first two dances."

"Heavens, he must have flown here to be so beforehand in asking."

"He came on horseback."

"Alone?"

"Yes, quite alone."

"Mr. Bradford did not accompany him?"

"Mr. Bradford is gone to Town. Lord Marcheek says he intends to bring to Cantywell several of his acquaintance—a number of fashionable ladies and unmarried gentlemen."

Although Cassandra was disappointed, she was also relieved. Mr. Bradford's absence guaranteed that she would not have to squirm under his enigmatic gaze.

"I am glad he is gone," Julia declared. "Marcheek says he is dashed interfering."

"Is he? He seems affable enough."

"You must learn that not everybody is what he seems, Cassie. Lord Marcheek says that though

Mr. Bradford may appear pleasant, he has often come between him and his amusements. We must be careful, he says, or he will stand in the way.''

"Stand in the way of what?"

"Of our plan."

Alerted, Cassandra looked at her sister.

"Well, don't you want to know what it is?" Julia asked conspiratorially. "It is very good fun, I think, and Lord Marcheek agrees. Even you, Cassie, as practical and dignified as you are, must be sensible of the adventure in it."

In spite of herself, Cassandra was deeply curious. "Tell me what it is," she said.

"On the night of the ball, Lord Marcheek will wear a mask of white satin. He has described it to me. It is trimmed in fur and has devilish eyes that come to a point."

An image of the mask rose before Cassandra and she inhaled.

"I shall wear a mask of scarlet and hold in my hand a rose. He will come to me to claim his dances and take me to the head of the line. We shall be the liveliest dancers in the room."

Cassandra swallowed. Her sister was right—she was exceedingly sensible of the adventure in the plan.

In a rapturous whisper, Julia continued, "At the stroke of midnight, we shall each steal away from the ballroom and meet in the library."

Cassandra scarcely dared imagine the words and looks which would pass between her sister, who, for all her brazenness, was as unworldly as it was possible to be, and his lordship, who, from all she had heard, was a thoroughgoing flirt. She began to be afraid for Julia.

"Do you not think it very good fun?" Julia exclaimed, laughing.

Coming to her, Cassandra said softly, "Good fun for the heroine of a novel, perhaps, but not the daughter of a clergyman."

"And why not? I am sure I am as entitled to amuse myself as anybody. More so, for I am suffocating for want of a little amusement."

"Dear Julia, I do understand, but you cannot meet Lord Marcheek. It will look very bad if you should be seen."

"I shall take care not to be seen. But I must see him alone so that I may have the opportunity of securing his heart. He is already half in love with me, you know. He may wish to kiss me, and if he does, I may let him, providing he says what is proper."

"It could be the ruin of you."

"It could be the making of me, you mean, for I shall be a marchioness one day, mark my words. But never fear. I shall not look down my nose at you, though you will be my inferior."

"Oh, Julia, I doubt he will marry you."

Affronted, Julia enquired whether she was in his lordship's confidence.

"Of course I am not," Cassandra replied, "but you know it is both immoral and imprudent to put your reputation at risk in such a manner. If you should be discovered, you will mortify Papa and break poor Mama's heart."

"You think that because you are drab and tiresome, everyone else ought to be, as well. I ought to have known you would not understand someone of my nature. I am not like you, Cassie. I require adventure. I shall go distracted with boredom if I do not have it."

"It does not matter what I think. The fact is that you expect your reckless behaviour to end in marriage, and it will not. It will be for nothing."

"Lord Marcheek has sworn to conduct himself with perfect propriety."

"Have you thought that he might mean merely to see how many kisses he can persuade you to part with, and then, when he has had his triumph, he will leave and forget you?"

Irritably, Julia said, "I ought never to have told you."

"I beg you, give up this scheme."

Julia walked to the glass and considered. "What colour ought my gown to be? White, I suppose, or perhaps yellow."

Cassandra grew firm. "I shall be obliged to inform Mama and Papa of your plan. They shall stop you from doing what must harm you—and all of us. They will keep you at home on the night of the ball.''

Julia laughed. ''Well, I shall simply say that you are jealous of my new gown and wish to keep me from showing it off.''

Angry though she was, Cassandra suppressed a reply. She was obliged to acknowledge to herself that she was indeed jealous, that meeting a masked nobleman at midnight during a ball was as thrilling a prospect as anything she had ever experienced outside her private imaginary world. Still, she would not let a few pangs of envy prevent her from doing what she knew to be right.

''I shall not say a word if you will tell Lord Marcheek that you cannot meet him. But if you persist, I shall be forced to speak.''

''You may speak to your heart's content. I shall point out to Mama that you wished to have Lord Marcheek for yourself and when you saw that he preferred me, you said what you said out of spite.''

Cassandra knew, as all the world knew, that because she was the beauty of the family, Julia was the centre of her mother's fondest hopes. Seeing her well married was the chief purpose of Mrs. Vickery's life. Consequently, she indulged Julia as she never indulged the eight who had followed, and the upshot was that the eldest Miss Vickery was as selfish and mulish as it was possible to be. Cassandra had little hope of being believed if she told her sister's secret.

Julia eyed Cassandra slyly. "You need not be jealous, you know, for though you cannot have Lord Marcheek, you can have someone else, someone who even now waits below."

"I have a visitor?"

"Yes, indeed, that is why I came—to fetch you."

"You said nothing about a visitor."

"I'm afraid I'd forgotten all about him, poor fellow. He is so easily forgotten."

Cassandra put her hand to her forehead and closed her eyes, for though Julia's description was brief, it was enough to tell her that Ned Bumpers had come to call, as though she did not have enough to plague her already.

Mrs. Vickery was eager for her second daughter to make the most of this visit from her long-time admirer and was disappointed when Cassandra entered the parlour appearing even more reserved than usual. Ned Bumpers's adoring looks were thrown away, for she would not so much as look at him. She would not sit on the same side of the room with him, much less on the same sofa, and would certainly have denied his petition for two dances at the Cantywell ball had not Mrs. Vickery stepped in and answered "Yes, so delighted," before a refusal could be uttered.

"Papa will let me borrow the plow horses so that I may call for you in the carriage," Ned said. As he spoke, his head jutted forward like a chicken's.

Cassandra nodded coolly. "I wish you and your father would not put yourselves to so much trouble."

"Trouble? I daresay, I like nothing so much as troubling myself about you, Miss Cassandra." On this, he beamed at her mother. He thrust his chin forward so often that Cassandra could scarcely keep from thinking of poultry.

"I was thinking," Cassandra ventured, "that I may not go to the Cantywell ball. I am given to understand that balls are tedious affairs, and as I much prefer reading a book to dancing, perhaps I ought to stay at home and help Nurse look after the children."

Her mother fixed her with an eye of steel and said, "You have already promised Mr. Bumpers his two dances. You cannot disappoint him now. Nor can you disappoint Lord Cantywell, for I am certain he would be desolate if you were to absent yourself. For that matter, you cannot disappoint me. You know it gives me no end of pleasure to see my girls dancing and amusing themselves."

"I would not wish to press Miss Cassandra to

do anything she finds dull,'' Ned said anxiously. ''Then she would be angry with me, and my Papa woud be angry with me if I made her angry with me. I cannot abide it when people are angry with me.''

''Then you must not permit Miss Cassandra to renege on her promise of two dances,'' said Mrs. Vickery with a thin smile, ''for then *I* shall be angry with you.''

This threat effectively put an end to Ned Bumpers's gallantry. After sitting in heavy silence for ten minutes, he rose and left Cassandra to the blandishments of her mother. These consisted of a lengthy disquisition on her duty to catch Ned Bumpers, who was the son of a gentleman, who lived on an allowance of three hundred a year and who was one day to inherit a fine house, good farm lands and an additional seven hundred per annum.

''But Mama, he looks like a rooster.''

''Cassandra Vickery! You are no prize yourself. You are fortunate to have attached the only man in the county who would value a wife who is ordinary-looking and dull.''

Cassandra blushed and said no more.

As soon as her mother released her, she returned to the attic chamber to find it empty. Seating herself at the little writing table, she tried to think what to do. There was no telling to what foolish lengths Julia would go in her quest to snare his lordship. She was a mixture of ignorance and wilfulness and was determined to escape the tedium of Hampshire through any means. Unlike herself, Cassandra thought, Julia was not content to escape in imagination, and therefore was capable of the greatest indiscretion. She might even go so far, Cassandra feared, as to consent to an elopement. How to stop her before she went too far—that was the difficulty.

The following evening, Mrs. Vickery gave a party to which the inmates of Cantywell were invited, along with Mr. and Mrs. Bumpers and Ned. Cassandra was surprised when Mr. Bradford walked into the drawing-room with his uncle. Because he had sought her face the instant he entered, he noted her surprise and remarked on it to her as they went to sit down to cards.

"I was told you had gone to Town," she said. "I did not expect to see you for some time."

"I went only for a day."

"And have you brought with you a bevy of fine ladies and gentlemen to attend your uncle's ball?"

"A strange question. What made you think so?"

"I was told that that was your reason for going up to Town."

"Your informant, whoever she was, was in error."

"My informant was your cousin. My sister told me what he had said of your journey."

His eyes narrowed. "I hope you are too wise to be taken in by my cousin," he said. "He is a delightful fellow, but not a word he says is to be believed."

Cassandra tried to smile at this, though her heart sank. "I am given to understand that he is a most honourable gentleman."

Laughing, he said, "*Honourable?* Your informant cannot be my cousin in this instance. Marcheek is a perfect rogue where the ladies are concerned, but even he would not hoax you so abominably."

Heartsick, Cassandra looked at the table where Julia and Marcheek were betting high. Their laughter was loud enough to attract the attention of the other guests. Cassandra remarked a number of them glancing at Julia, rolling their eyes and exchanging whispers. By the expressions they wore, Cassandra judged that the whispers were not of a kindly nature. When she looked again at her companion, she was startled to find him studying her closely. "What is the matter?" he asked.

His discernment awed her somewhat. Taking a breath, she assumed a light air and said, "I was merely wondering what sent you to Town yesterday if it was not to bring back a party of merrymakers."

"Masks," he said. "I procured a selection of masks, so that none of my uncle's good neighbours should be obliged to refuse his invitation for want of the proper attire."

"That was most kind of you." She smiled at him.

He approached nearer and said quietly, "Am I to understand that you have forgiven me for what you were pleased to call my 'mockery'?"

Colouring, she said, "Perhaps I spoke too heatedly."

"And will you now acknowledge that it was kind in me to fetch your pretty pictures from the ditch-water? You never did thank me, you know."

Mortified, she did not know how to reply.

"You will be pleased to know that my valet forgave me and did not quit my employ, but to keep him, I was obliged to tell a small fib. He believes I soiled my boots to rescue your person, not your paintings. If he had known what it was I was truly after, he would have given me notice on the spot."

"You ought not to have risked your valet's displeasure. The paintings were spoiled beyond saving."

"Ah, were all of them spoiled? Nothing could be saved? What a pity. I hope this calamity does not discourage you from attempting to paint again."

Seizing her opportunity, Cassandra assumed a

dejected aspect and said, "It is excessively discouraging. I do not think I shall ever recover. Therefore, I have made up my mind to renounce art from this time forward."

He looked startled. Clearly, she thought with satisfaction, he had not expected his teasing to have such a serious consequence. "It is fortunate you got your daisy when you did," she said, "for it assuredly is the last expression of the artistic impulse which will ever fall from my brush."

Mr. Bradford would have protested warmly, but Ned Bumpers demanded Cassandra's attention.

"I vow," the young man declared to her, "you are angry with me. You have not said a word to me this night."

While Cassandra introduced the young man to him, Mr. Bradford looked him up and down. It was clear in an instant that the fellow was head over ears in love with Cassandra. He thrust his chin at her so often and so pathetically that he was either deeply in love or he suffered from the disorder known as St. Vitus's dance. As he was in every other regard a fine specimen of health, Mr. Bradford concluded that his unusual demeanour must be ascribed to violent passion.

Cassandra's feelings were not so clear. Amiably and patiently enough, she reassured Ned that she was not angry with him, but whether she returned his regard, Mr. Bradford could not tell. He sincerely hoped not.

"What cause have I to be angry with you?" Cassandra asked Ned. "You are one of my oldest friends. We were in leading-strings together."

"Yes, but it is my fault you are obliged to attend the ball. And I know you dislike it. You wished to stay at home and read a book, and though I cannot understand a preference for books, which always send me to snoring in an instant, I do not like to be the cause of your doing what you do not like to do."

Mr. Bradford fixed her with a stern eye. "You do not wish to attend the ball, Miss Cassandra? But I felt certain it was exactly to your taste, especially as you were the one who first approved the suggestion of a masked ball."

Ned cried out, "You approved it, Miss Cassandra? I do not understand. Do you mean to attend or not? I must know what I am to do with the first two dances. If I cannot have them with you, I must go and hunt up someone else. Papa will be angry with me if I make a muddle of the business."

Trapped, she replied, "You already have my promise for the first two dances, and I mean to keep it."

Relieved, he performed a series of head flutters which caused Cassandra to recollect that morning's visit to the hen coop. She became so engrossed in watching him that she was startled when Mr. Bradford enquired, ''And may I have your promise for the second two dances?''

Never before had Cassandra been noticed by two gentlemen in the same evening. Indeed, she generally found herself ignored, except when her mother poked her with her fan and insisted she exert herself in company. She confessed to herself that she was not entirely sorry to have been deprived of an evening alone with a book.

Her hesitation in replying prompted Mr. Bradford to repeat the invitation. ''But,'' he added, ''perhaps the second two are already spoken for. Perhaps you are engaged to my cousin for those dances.''

Cassandra looked at him in wonder. It seemed that Mr. Bradford was blind to the flirtation his cousin was conducting with her sister. He actually thought that Lord Marcheek might have asked her to dance! For some unaccountable reason, his misapprehension pleased her. She smiled, and even though her mother was not there at the moment to speak for her, she took a breath, boldly met his eyes and granted his application.

Chapter Four

The Masked Ball

While the valet bustled to get him dressed for the ball, Mr. Bradford pondered the mystery of Miss Cassandra Vickery. Her serene expression reminded him of the face on a mosaic he had discovered in India, which when he had seen it, had struck him with its exquisiteness. There was, at times, a hint of wistfulness in her expression, as well, which suggested unformed yearnings, and more than a hint of passion in her grey eyes. The manner in which she wore her hair, in longer and more severe plaits than was strictly the fashion, gave her a quaint air, and the creamy smoothness of her complexion inspired him to wonder what it might be like to touch her cheek.

He grew restless at these thoughts, provoking much anxiety in his valet, who quarrelled with his

master's cravat and could not bend it precisely to
his will. Meanwhile, Mr. Bradford recalled Cassandra's stunning announcement that she had given
up painting. Her renunciation displeased him so
much that he lost patience with the valet's fastid-
iousness. The man was obliged to follow him from
the looking-glass to the table to the window, and
to plead with him to stand still. But Mr. Bradford
was too angry to remain planted in one spot. More
than once he had seen women with great gifts sti-
fled by marriage, childbearing, domesticity, pov-
erty and the world's indifference. The same fate
might overtake Miss Cassandra if something were
not done. Her discouragement might be so extreme
as to induce her to accept a proposal of marriage
from Ned Bumpers, who appeared a pleasant
enough chap but not at all suited to her tempera-
ment. She would not be the first young lady to seek
escape from the world's unkindness in the safety
of marriage. Once she had taken that momentous
step, however, she would certainly never paint
again, for what her own natural modesty and self-
doubt did not do to prevent her, her husband's in-
anities and the demands of her children and household would. He determined that when next he saw
her he would speak to her, change her mind, make
her see, regardless of how much she protested, the
absurdity and tragedy of her renunciation. If he did
nothing else while he sojourned in Hampshire, he

would persuade Miss Cassandra Vickery to take up her brushes again.

Unfortunately, he was the last man to inspire her to persevere in her art. She was wary of him and never spent a quarter hour in his company without evading even his most innocuous questions. The more he endeavoured to ingratiate himself, the more she kept him at arm's length, and he had no one to blame for it but himself. He had shown too much interest in her painting, and now she did not trust him. However, he meant to remedy the situation that very evening, when he claimed his dances with her.

By the time the valet was satisfied with the folds of the cravat, Mr. Bradford had been dressed to perfection. He wore a blue coat and silver waistcoat. His dark hair had been combed à la Brutus. He peered at himself one final time in the glass and affixed his loo mask. It was black and unadorned and covered the entire upper half of his face. When he smiled, it lent him a rakish air. He had never seen himself look quite so dashing, and he hoped such an aspect would do much to rouse Miss Cassandra Vickery's interest.

Lord Marcheek strode into his chamber then, attired in a green brocade coat, lace cravat and a mask of white satin. He would certainly have appeared the quintessence of a romantic hero had he not sighed and pouted so wretchedly.

"By the look of you, cousin," Mr. Bradford said as he sat in a high-backed chair, "you are either ill or in love."

Marcheek sank onto the bed and shook his head. "Dash it all, James, I am a vast deal of both."

"You are not going to beg off from the ball, I trust. My uncle has gone to great expense and trouble over it, and you will not disappoint him."

"I'm afraid I've got myself in a bit of a scrape."

"You cannot be fleeing another jealous husband so soon. You have only just arrived in Hampshire."

"It is worse, much worse, alas."

"You have not made an assignation with Lady Loveless, I hope, for if you have, do not expect me to collect the pieces of your corpse. I wash my hands of you."

Marcheek sighed. "I might have done better to continue to amuse myself with women who are shackled to husbands, for though husbands have a disagreeable propensity to carry pistols and aim them at my head, they are far less alarming than an unmarried female."

"You had better tell me—who is she?"

"You may well ask."

"She must be extraordinary if she makes you nostalgic for the sight of a jealous husband's pistol. Yet you have not indicated, in my hearing at least, that you have lost your heart. Let me see, which of the maidens we have met might have caught your fancy? All of them, I think.''

"Dash and damn,'' Marcheek mourned, ''she is the prettiest, slyest, most delectable female a fellow could hope to find in this desolate part of the world.''

"Ah, you refer to the barmaid at the Horse's Head. I remember you thought her irresistible, and she returned the compliment.''

Offended, Marcheek replied, ''I assure you, the female of whom I speak is a most respectable young lady. That is the difficulty.''

Mr. Bradford grew alert. This respectable young lady might well be Miss Vickery, he thought. Marcheek had dangled after her pretty foolishly of late. If Julia was indeed the lady in question, then Cassandra would be affected, for the conduct of an older sister would necessarily reflect on the younger. He began to consider how he might prevent any harm to Cassandra's reputation and peace of mind. The best means, he concluded, was to warn Marcheek off without seeming to. ''You are so accustomed to meeting the other sort of lady,'' he said, '' that you scarcely know how to behave with the respectable variety, and you want my advice. Well, I advise you to be careful and to refrain from any show of particularity.''

"It is worse than you know,'' Marcheek said

with a sigh. "You see, I have promised to meet her, in secret."

At this, Mr. Bradford sat forward. It occurred to him that the lady they spoke of could as well be Cassandra as Miss Vickery. He recollected the exchange he had witnessed between his cousin and Cassandra at Tickleton Farm—their mutual glance, their handshake. He was on the point of asking straight out who the young lady was but hesitated, reluctant to let slip to such a fellow as Marcheek the least hint that he was interested in the younger Miss Vickery. Nevertheless, he was determined to do what he could to prevent a secret meeting. To that end, he said ominously, "I caution you, do not meet her. You will regret it if you do."

Marcheek paled. "Yes, I know, and I have no desire to be married these fifty years at least."

"If that is the case, then you will change your mind about meeting the lady."

"But it is all arranged. I am to meet her in the library at the stroke of midnight."

"The stroke of midnight? I hope she hooted with laughter at such gothic nonsense."

"Not at all. She was prodigiously pleased. Women like that sort of thing, you know, and I am always happy to oblige."

Suppressing his temper, Mr. Bradford said, "If the lady is respectable, as you say, then she will be better off if you do not keep the appointment."

"She will be in a dreadful taking if I fail her."

"I assure you, she will be even angrier if you spend an hour with her alone in the library at midnight and then do not engage yourself to her in marriage. And you will be quite angry with her if she lands you in the courts with a suit for breach of promise. Respectable ladies do not take these matters lightly, you know." If the lady in question were indeed Miss Cassandra, Mr. Bradford trusted that this dire prophecy would put an end to Marcheek's infatuation with her.

His lordship threw himself on the bed and pouted. "Dash it all, I was a fool to say I would meet her."

"Yes, and now you must pay the piper."

"I'm dashed, James. You have saved me from Loveless's pistol only to see me shot to pieces by a country girl, for when I do not appear in the library tonight, I shall be good as dead."

Mr. Bradford smiled. "Yes, but at least you will not be married."

Arm in arm, the Vickery daughters entered the ballroom at Cantywell behind their parents. Julia's scarlet mask was trimmed in gold filigree. Cassandra's was made of peacock-blue feathers which swept gracefully towards her temples. Her grey eyes shone through the mask. Her chestnut hair was swept high off her neck, and she wore a short puffed-sleeved white muslin which, when she lowered her fan, revealed a low bodice trimmed in blue ribbon.

The ballroom at Cantywell had known such little use that the housekeeper, Mrs. Clapshew, had feared it would not do. However, under the lady's fastidious direction, it had become almost handsome. The azure ornamented ceiling curved upwards to a high arc in the centre, from which hung a long, circular brass chandelier. Near the fireplace stood an array of chairs for those who preferred conversation to dancing. Near one corner, the musicians played a lively reel. The doors to the terrace were thrown open to give a view of the starlit night. Couples in masks were already engaged in dancing. The two Misses Vickery fanned themselves and waited for their partners to claim them.

"I have forgotten who everybody is," Julia whispered. "Is it not wonderfully mysterious."

"There is Mr. Pinch," Cassandra said.

"Is that indeed Mr. Pinch?"

"Of course. Even if I did not know what mask he was to wear, I should know him by the knob of his knees."

"Why, you are right, Cassie. Mr. Pinch does have knobby knees. You are amazingly observant."

"I am observant enough to notice that you are carrying a red rose." The defiance that gleamed in her sister's eyes did not escape Cassandra, despite the scarlet mask. "I am afraid you mean to carry out this reckless plan of yours," she said.

"Oh, am I carrying a rose? How silly of me." Julia laughed gaily. "I promise, I have forgotten all about that idle notion of meeting Lord Marcheek."

Cassandra said earnestly, "Do be serious. Tell me that you have truly come to your senses."

"Certainly I have. I never had any intention of carrying out such a plan."

"You didn't?"

"I was merely hoaxing you. And you believed me. How very credulous you are, Cassie."

Cassandra tried to smile at the joke.

"Now, don't you feel foolish?"

"I feel uneasy. I wish we might go home."

"We cannot leave now," Julia declared. "Here is a partner to claim you for a dance."

Cassandra turned to see Ned clicking his heels in a bow. A green loo mask hid his face but did not disguise the persistent bob of his head.

He greeted the young ladies with an apology for disturbing their tête-à-tête. "I do hope you are not angry with me," he said. "I know that young ladies must have privacy when they confide their secrets to each other."

Julia gave him an insinuating smile, saying, "There is at least one member of my family who could never be angry with such a devilishly hand-some fellow as you, Mr. Bumpers.''

He screwed up his face in puzzlement. ''Really? I wonder who it could be.''

While he was mulling the answer to this riddle, Julia skipped off and was soon lost to view in the crowd. Cassandra wished she might follow her, for though Julia had taken her oath that she did not mean to meet his lordship, Cassandra did not be-lieve a word of it. Julia was more determined than ever, she suspected, to run to her doom, and Cas-sandra was more determined than ever to stop her.

''I cannot for the life of me think who it could be, unless it is your mother,'' Ned said. ''I expect your sister was quizzing me.''

''We had better dance,'' Cassandra told him.

He led her down to the set, and she soon found that there was little pleasure in the dance, for Ned contrived to find her toes with his feet on numerous occasions. At each crunch, he apologized and hoped she was not angry.

''Mr. Bumpers, if you persist in asking me whether I am angry, you will succeed in making me excessively angry with you.''

''Dear me, I detest it when anyone is angry with me. I shall endeavor to find the means of making it up to you, Miss Cassandra. I shall, indeed.''

''Do you mean that?''

''Certainly.''

"I know exactly how you may make it up to me, if you mean what you say."

"Of course I mean what I say. How can you doubt me?" He jutted his chin forward, a little affronted.

"What I have to ask requires cleverness and determination."

"Put me to the test!"

"Go and find my sister. Do not let her see you. Tell me everything you observe and overhear."

Abruptly, he stopped dancing. His head bobbed furiously. "You wish me to spy on Miss Vickery?"

Inhaling for courage, she answered, "Yes."

"I thought perhaps you would like a trinket of some sort, or perhaps a proposal of marriage. Papa says that women are very fond of being proposed to."

"I should much prefer to have you spy on my sister."

He scratched his head. "Can it be that Papa was wrong? Papa is never wrong."

Cassandra pushed him in the direction of the crowd at the entrance. "Oh, please, go and find her. Go quickly."

He took a step and then was back. "Do you think I ought to wear the mask?"

"Yes," she said and shooed him off.

Again, he was back. "You promise you will not

be angry with me any longer if I oblige you in this?''

''I will forgive you with all my heart, but you must hurry. I do not see her anywhere. Where can she have disappeared to?''

Once more he returned, much to her despair. ''What of my dances? We have not completed the two dances you promised me.''

''When you return, I shall be entirely yours.''

The grin that flashed below the mask told her that she had won her point. ''I am off,'' he announced and bobbed purposefully towards the entrance.

She watched him go, too immersed in an agony of apprehension to note the line of dancers forming nearby, or Mr. Bradford, who approached very near and startled her by saying into her ear, ''I see your partner has deserted you. Perhaps I might be permitted to take his place.''

Mr. Bradford had seen her enter with her family and had not taken his eyes off her since. He smiled to see her in a peacock-blue mask. Earlier in the week he had sent a parcel of masks to the rectory, expressly asking that the feathered one be given to Miss Cassandra. She wore it well, he thought, as he had expected she would.

With a nod, she laid her hand upon his arm so that he might lead her onto the floor. The violins lilted; the chandelier glowed; the dance began, and he felt Cassandra's searching eyes on his face.

"Lord Marcheek?" she asked. "Is it you?"

Mr. Bradford set his teeth. "No, indeed, only his cousin."

"There is a great resemblance between you. Because of the masks, it is difficult to tell you apart."

"Let me assist you. Marcheek's mask is white; mine, black."

"Yes, I recall now. He was to wear a mask of white satin, turned up at the eyes and trimmed in fur. How could I have forgotten?"

All at once he looked grim. He clasped her hand tighter as she walked in a circle under his arm. "I expect Lord Marcheek told you how you might recognize him."

She tried unsuccessfully to loosen his grip. "Everybody knows what masks are to be worn and by whom. My father stipulated as much when he approved the masked ball."

He stopped a moment, nearly oversetting the line of dancers. "Miss Cassandra, did you or did you not agree to meet my cousin at the stroke of midnight in the library?"

Pulling her hand away, Cassandra said, "I do not see that my meetings are any affair of yours."

Swiftly, he propelled her from the floor to a pillar. She backed against it, breathing hard. He took her hand.

"Let me go," she commanded, unable to break his firm grip.

"You would do better to keep to your daisies." His voice was low and granite hard.

For an instant, their eyes locked.

They might have held each other in that manner for the rest of the night if Ned Bumpers had not come along to say, "Miss Cassandra, I have done as you asked." Innocently, he jutted his chin in her direction, then in Mr. Bradford's, and noticing at last that the two continued fixed in an icy stare, he enquired, "Oh, have I interrupted? I apologize. I hope you are not angry with me."

Mr. Bradford was oblivious to the intruder. "Be careful," he whispered to Cassandra. Suddenly he released her, bowed curtly and left her side.

Seething, Cassandra watched him go. When she turned at last to Ned, she said breathlessly, "He is insufferable."

"Who is he? I thought perhaps it might be Lord Marcheek."

"Never mind that. What have you discovered?"

"I found Miss Julia engaged in conversation with a gentleman."

"What gentleman?"

"How the deuce should I know? I cannot be expected to remember everybody's mask."

"What sort of mask was it?"

"It was white, satin perhaps, fur trimmed, very elegant."

"Oh, heavens, I was afraid of that."

"You are not angry with me, are you?"

"No, not with you. Tell me what you saw."

"I saw little, but I heard much. I heard her say that she would rendezvous with him at the appointed time."

"What did he say?"

"Not a great deal. He was coughing and choking."

"Perhaps he will be too ill to meet her."

"She seemed to think he would not. Before taking leave of him, she kissed his cheek. I confess, I was quite shocked at her conduct."

"Thank you, Ned. I am most grateful. If you wish to dance now, I am at liberty. I only wish I knew what to do."

Mr. Bradford made for the library, thinking to find his cousin there, but the room was dark and empty. In the ballroom again, he scanned the crowd in vain for a white satin mask. Vexed at not finding it, he strode outside onto the terrace and breathed in the fresh night air. On the third breath, he observed Marcheek, skulking by the foot of the stairs between two potted junipers.

In a flash, he was down the steps and had his cousin by the collar. "What the devil do you mean by making a secret assignation with Miss Cassandra Vickery?''

Marcheek's mouth flapped, but as he was being choked at the moment, he was unable to vouchsafe a coherent reply.

''I did not think you had sunk so low as this.'' Disgusted, Mr. Bradford pushed Marcheek away from him, causing him to stagger.

Hands at his throat, Marcheek rasped, ''It wasn't Miss Cassandra I was to meet. It was the other one.''

''What other one?''

''Miss Julia Vickery.''

Mr. Bradford studied him skeptically. ''You meant to meet the sister?''

''Dash it, James, she has been my principal flirt since I arrived in Hampshire. I thought you had noticed. Everybody else has.''

''Yes, I noticed, but I did not think that even you could sustain a flirtation with a vapid creature who does nothing but complain and pout.''

''Well, I confess I did fancy Miss Cassandra for a time, but I would not dream of making such an invitation to her.''

''And why not? She is superior to her sister in every way.''

''That's as may be, but I have had the notion for some days that you rather fancied her yourself, and I do have some scruples, you know, not many, but one or two where my family are concerned.''

Mr. Bradford calmed a bit and brushed his cousin's coat where he had wrinkled it.

''I declare, James, you ought to let me put a word in Miss Cassandra's ear on your behalf. I should like to further your cause. It's the least I can do, given all the escapades I've survived owing to your intervention.''

''If you wish to assist me, you will take your oath that you will forever spare Miss Cassandra and her family the mortification of having a relation who willingly meets in secret with scoundrels.''

''By *scoundrels*, I hope you are not alluding to me. I merely wish to assist you in your suit. I can be dashed persuasive with the ladies, you know.''

''You can help best by not helping.''

''I should be the soul of discretion, and though you do not admit it, you do need assistance, for you have grown dashed fond of the girl in a short space.''

Unwilling to unfold even a hint of his true feelings to such a fellow as Marcheek, Mr. Bradford changed the subject. ''What are you doing out here, anyway? You ought to be dancing so that my uncle can see how pleased you are with his ball.''

''If you must know, I am taking your advice. As I do not intend to keep my appointment in the library at midnight, I am obliged to hide from Miss Julia. Should she find me again, I shall be lost. She trapped me in the gallery earlier, and I nearly found myself swearing to be forever true.'' He shuddered.

''Perhaps you had better meet her in the library as planned. It would be best to explain to her that you regret having agreed to a meeting and will not suggest anything so improper again. Then you may tell her that you do not intend to marry her or anybody else for many years to come.''

Taking a step back, Marcheek cried, ''Why on Earth should I do such a thing as that?''

''Because you owe her an explanation. You owe it to yourself to meet her face to face like a man and tell her the truth.''

''Dash it, James, you have seen me on the run often enough to know I never meet a woman face to face or tell her the truth if I can help it.''

''My dear cousin, you are a coward.''

''I'm glad you understand the situation.''

''Yes, but you do not. If you fail to meet Miss Julia, if you merely decline to appear, she will not know that you have in fact changed your mind. She will invent a hundred excuses in your favour, and when you next see her, she will press you to set a new time for another meeting.''

Marcheek's hands flew to his cheeks. His jaw went slack. He gazed at Mr. Bradford with a pathetic expression and said, "You are right, James. She will be after me again at the first opportunity. Well, there is only one thing for it. I shall have to leave Hampshire altogether. We must both leave at once."

"I have no intention of leaving. If you are too pigeon-hearted to tell the young lady the truth, then I shall have to do it for you."

"You?"

"Here," Mr. Bradford instructed. "Give me your coat and mask. The young lady will hear the truth from a gentleman in a white satin mask. That ought to satisfy all parties concerned, and then we shall have done with this nonsense."

Chapter Five

At the Stroke of Midnight

Mr. Bradford escorted his cousin into the shadows of a topiary hedge so that they might exchange clothing without being seen from the terrace.

"Give you my coat?" Marcheek protested. "But my tailor took an entire day to fit it to me, and I had even thought of paying him for it one day."

"Give it here. You may put this on."

"You do not expect me to dress without the aid of a valet!"

Fixing his cousin with a stern eye, Mr. Bradford said, "I expect you to do exactly as you are told."

Marcheek eased a step away and, clearing his throat, changed his tune. "I have always admired your excellent taste in coats, James, though I look a fright in smoked blue."

When they had both adjusted their new masks, Mr. Bradford glanced up at the terrace and found it empty. "It is safe now," he said. "We shall return to the drawing-room."

His cousin hung back. "But what if Miss Julia should see me? She may upbraid me. She may fall into hysterics. She may kill herself, or, worse, she may kill me."

Mr. Bradford smiled. "Calm yourself. You are not Lord Marcheek any longer. Miss Vickery will ignore you completely, just as she ignores me. You are, after all, Mr. James Bradford, that well-travelled collector, that man of the world, that gentleman known for rescuing a coward when he is about to receive an attack on his pate—or his bachelorhood. I, on the other hand, am Lord Marcheek, so that if she has anything disagreeable to say, she may say it to me."

Shaking his head, Marcheek said darkly, "I hope you know what you are about, for if something should go amiss, I do not know who shall be obliged to rescue whom."

As soon as Cassandra saw Mr. Bradford come into the ballroom from the terrace, she put herself in his way, determined that he should know how dissatisfied she was with his late behaviour. He was forced to stop and greet her, after which he would have hied himself as far from her as he could, she saw, but she stopped him with, "Have you forgotten our dances, sir?"

He regarded her blankly.

"So, not only do you accuse me of the most imprudent conduct, not only do you squeeze my wrist until it smarts, not only do you presume to hurl warnings and threats in my face, but you pretend you never asked my promise for two dances."

Astounded, he replied, "Dash it, that is to say, zounds! Did I do all that? If so, then I am a bounder. Forgetting our dances is unforgivable, and therefore, I shall not be so presumptuous as to apologize. I have no right to call myself a gentleman. You have every reason never to speak to me again."

A little mollified, she said, "In point of fact, an apology is all I require."

"Oh, in that case, I beg your pardon." He bowed and brought her hand to his lips.

She had never known the gentleman to be so gallant. It gave her courage to venture, "Mr. Bradford, may I speak frankly?"

"Certainly."

"Judging by what you said earlier, I'm afraid you do not think very highly of me. Not that your opinion of me matters, of course, but one does not like to be falsely accused."

"Oh, dear, did I do that, too?"

"You thought I was about to meet Lord Marcheek in the library, didn't you? You actually believed that of me.''

"Well, I can understand your wishing to meet him. He is a handsome fellow and quite devastatingly charming.''

"He is a blockhead.''

"I say, that's coming it a bit strong. I am dashed fond of him, you know.''

"He is a blockhead if he imagines I will allow him to ruin my sister. You see, it is my sister who plans to meet him, not I. I hope you are undeceived now.''

"I assure you, Lord Marcheek does not wish to ruin anybody. He wants only to be left in peace. If the ladies did not plague him to make promises he is incapable of keeping, he would not fall into half so many scrapes as he does.''

"Do you really think he does not wish to ruin her? Oh, I should be grateful to believe it.''

"I can vouch for it. No one knows him as well as I do.''

"I wish I could be certain. I wish I could hear his promise with my own ears.''

"In that case, you must go to him. You must put the case before him with all the reason and earnestness at your command.''

"But I scarcely know the gentleman.''

"Then there is no time like the present to improve your acquaintance.''

"What am I to say to him?"

"You must tell him how much you admire him. You must say that you depend on his good nature and nobleness of heart to save your sister and your family from scandal and destruction."

"I would not have the face to tell such lies."

"Oh. Well, then, you must simply ask him not to meet your sister."

"Do you think he will give up the scheme simply by being asked?"

"Absolutely, especially once he hears your pretty speech. I vow, he will not be able to resist you."

Struck by this suggestion, she considered.

"Miss Cassandra, would you grant me one small favour?"

"You have been so helpful to me, Mr. Bradford, I could not deny you one small favour."

He smiled broadly. "Excellent. When you do speak to my cousin, be sure and tell him it was I who sent you!"

Mr. Bradford located a candle to illumine enough of the library to prevent his colliding with the furniture. As a fire had not been lit, it was cold, and as there was the tiniest sliver of a quarter moon in the sky, little brightness was gained from the tall narrow window. After adjusting his mask for the thousandth time, he removed his pocket watch and noted by the dim light of the candle that it was two minutes short of midnight. He hoped Miss Julia would not be late, for the fur trim on the white satin mask tickled his nose. More than that, he wished to conclude this business as swiftly as possible so that he might resume his own identity and claim his dances with Miss Cassandra.

It gratified him to hear the door creak and to see a lady peek inside, but his pleasure vanished when he saw that she wore a mask of peacock-blue feathers. What the deuce was Miss Cassandra doing there, he wished to know. More to the point, how was he going to get rid of her before her sister arrived?

She closed the door quietly and came inside. He was aware that flickers of candlelight shadowed her dress, enhancing her graceful form. "Lord Marcheek," she said forthrightly, though he detected a hint of trembling in her voice, "I do not know whether you recollect me or my mask. It is Cassandra Vickery."

Assuming his cousin's raffish air, he replied, "Madam, I am dashed if I have ever invited a lady to leave my side, but I must ask you to do so at once. I am expecting a visitor who will not wish to be seen. I am certain you understand."

"Oh, I do understand. But Mr. Bradford said I must come."

"Did you say 'Mr. Bradford'?"

"Yes. He said to tell you he had sent me."

Between his teeth he replied, "My cousin is too dashed fond of interfering in my dashed concerns. I vow, next time he wishes to rescue me from the hands of a madman, I shall insist that he leave me to my own dashed devices. If I wish to have my dashed brains shot out, it is my affair and none of his."

She moved closer to him. "Please, I do not wish to cause a quarrel between you and your cousin. I have come to ask you—to beg you—to give up this plan to meet here with my sister."

He glanced at his pocket watch once more. "Nothing easier. I shall gladly give it up. And now, I bid you good-night."

A silence ensued, during which he noted that the seconds were ticking away and that although he had granted her request and said his farewell, Cassandra was not any nearer the door than before. He noted, too, that her white dress gave her neck and shoulders a rosy glow, over which the candlelight played hypnotically.

Again she moved closer, so close, in fact, that as she spoke, he felt her sweet breath on his cheek.

"I did not expect such quick agreement," she said, "and, I confess, I am uncertain as to what to do. I do not know whether I may trust you."

He put a gloved finger to her chin. "You may trust me to take care of everything."

It struck him that she was dangerously near and that if he did not step away instantly, he would kiss her. He had every intention of virtuously stepping away and nobly refraining from kissing her, but when he saw the door open and Julia look in, he thought the better part of valour might well be indiscretion. As the clock struck the first note of twelve, he slipped his hand round Cassandra's waist, pulled her firmly to him and planted a kiss on her lips. Then the second stroke of twelve sounded.

His object was to blast Julia's hopes by showing Lord Marcheek locked in intimate embrace with another female. This purpose was soon forgotten, however, in the response he elicited from Cassandra. At first she seemed too astonished to do more than freeze in his arms. Next she put her hands to his breast in an effort to resist. Then her resistance waned and she went limp, giving herself up to the press of his arms around her and the sensation of his kiss. And finally, she threw her arms about his neck and sought his mouth with a fervour that matched his own.

Though his surprise was considerable, it was still less than his delight. Had his lips not already been occupied, he would have smiled a smile of deep pleasure. Instead, he held Cassandra fast and kissed her as though he might never have another opportunity. The sensation of her kiss put him in mind of her painting, in which she seemed to throw off all restraint and let her brush freely flow. Her ardour stirred him so powerfully that as he caressed her, he began to think he would never be able to let her go.

In all this confusion of bliss and amazement, of gentleness and force, of kissing and embracing, Julia was utterly neglected. Because she was a young lady who never permitted herself to be neglected, she effectivelly summoned the others' attention by dint of shrieking at the top of her voice. This expedient succeeded in inducing Cassandra to pull free of the arms that held her and to back away, her hand to her lips, staring in anguish at her indignant sister.

Mr. Bradford, seeing that his plan had succeeded in shocking Julia, said in Marcheek's most offhand tone, "Well, I'm dashed if I ain't been caught."

"Oh, you are both contemptible!" Julia cried. "Worse than contemptible. Oh, I wish I knew a word bad enough for what you are. That is what comes of living a dreary country life—one never knows a word bad enough." She punctuated this speech with gurgles of fury.

"Julia, you misunderstand," Cassandra began. She put out her hands and approached her sister.

Narrowing her eyes, Julia shot back, "I understand perfectly. It is wicked of *me* to meet Lord

Marcheek in the library at midnight but *you* may do exactly as you please.''

Conscious and ashamed, Cassandra could not reply.

Mr. Bradford would have liked nothing better than to reassure Cassandra on the spot, but he dared not give himself away. In similar circumstances, he knew, his cousin would have excused himself at once, leaving the ladies to rip each other's throat out in private. Unwilling to leave Cassandra, however, he contented himself with saying, ''No need to make a dashed stir, is there?''

Julia hissed, ''I shall never forgive you. Either of you.''

Cassandra turned away and covered her face with her hands.

Bursting into tears, Julia cried, ''I shall not forget how I have been used this night. I shall make you sorry for this, I promise you,'' and stormed from the room.

For a time, Mr. Bradford observed Cassandra. If she wept, she did so with such restraint that she made no sound. Slowly, he approached her, standing near her back, wishing he might soothe her with a touch, but he lacked Marcheek's effrontery and, therefore, could merely commiserate with her in silence. After a time, he handed her a linen so that she might wipe her tears. Docilely, she took it but did not seem to know what use to make of it.

At last, she was sufficiently restored to face him. Her mask failed to hide her wet eyes. Desolate, she said, ''My sister is right. I have been guilty of the very thing I wished to prevent in her.''

Mr. Bradford could not let her blame herself. Kissing Cassandra had been the happiest of inspirations, in his estimation. It had not only been successful in driving off Julia, but it had been thoroughly pleasant. ''I am entirely at fault,'' he said as contritely as he could, which was not a great deal. ''I beg your pardon.''

She gazed at him in wonder. ''You beg my pardon?''

Realizing he had spoken out of character for Marcheek, he said quickly, ''I'm dashed to pieces if your sister does not soon find a proper object for her anger. She will direct it at me and forgive you. Sisters cannot long be angry.''

Cassandra cried, ''She may forgive me, but I shall never forgive myself.'' Stifling a sob, she hurried from the library.

As soon as he was alone, Mr. Bradford found his pleasure in the kiss begin to vanish. Disquiet and vexation overtook him as it hit him that Miss Cassandra's ardour had been roused not by Mr. James Bradford but by his incorrigible cousin, Marcheek. In Cassandra's view, she had kissed Denys Marcheek. It was Marcheek's lips she had reached for, Marcheek's arms she had clung to,

Marcheek's passion that had stirred hers. As himself, Mr. Bradford saw, he scarcely existed for her. If she knew who had really kissed her, she would probably grow prostrate with disappointment. Although he had never in his life envied his cousin's success with the ladies, he certainly did now.

When Cassandra returned to the ballroom, her mother greeted her with the news that Julia had been taken violently ill. They all must leave for the rectory, Mrs. Vickery said distractedly, as soon as the chaise could be brought round. With a bow of her head, Cassandra acquiesced. She could not wait to be home in her bed so that she might think. Unfortunately, it was a bed she shared with Julia.

The ride to Pilkingdown Rectory seemed the longest of Cassandra's life. Her sister regarded her from under lowered lashes and pinched her arm whenever she might do so without exciting her parents' notice. As soon as they alighted, the two sisters made for their attic room. They prepared for bed in thick silence and avoided looking at each other as they donned their nightshifts and caps. Their mother brought a bowl of broth to Julia, which she could not coax her to taste. "I shall go to bed, then," Mrs. Vickery said, sighing. "Perhaps you will eat your broth for Cassandra's sake if you will not do so for mine."

Ignoring her mother's entreaty, Julia slipped under the quilt and arranged herself stiffly on the pillow. Cassandra blew out the candle and climbed in beside her, keeping as far from her as she could. Within minutes, it occurred to her that no amount of distance and silence would soothe either Julia's wrath or her own conscience, and so she marshalled all her courage and said, "Oh, Julia, I have been very bad. You have every right to hate me. I thought I could spare you the humiliation of meeting with a known flirt under scandalous circumstances and ended by humiliating you and myself. I am so ashamed."

"You need not give it another thought," Julia said coolly.

Cassandra sat up. "Do you mean that?"

"If you wish to know whether I've told Mama, I haven't."

"What I wish to know is whether you can forgive me."

"Of course I forgive you, but you must promise to avoid Lord Marcheek in future."

Sighing, Cassandra wondered if she could keep such a promise. The gentleman's nearness had produced a powerful effect on her. Her cheeks flamed as the recollection of his touch rose in her imagination. Immediately, however, she banished the image. She must put the entire episode from her mind, she warned herself. Lord Marcheek was everything he was reputed to be and worse: a cunning, unprincipled, unfeeling flirt. Misery and despair lay in store for the woman who was foolish enough to succumb to his kisses. With all the strength of which she was mistress, she vowed, she would suppress the feeling he had roused in her, both for Julia's sake and her own. Accordingly, she told her sister in a near whisper, "I promise."

"Do you promise you will not put yourself in his way again?"

"I had little to do with him before tonight, and I believe I know better than to pursue such an acquaintance."

"You will not converse with him? You will not sit or stand near him, or give him any opportunity to speak to you?"

"I take my oath, Julia, I have not set my cap for Lord Marcheek. I am well aware that no further word may pass between us."

"I have never known you to lie."

"I have never lied to you, and I am not lying now."

"I expect you lack the imagination to lie."

Cassandra blushed.

"Well then, I forgive you," Julia declared.

For the first time since she had stepped into the library at Cantywell, Cassandra felt herself breathe. "You are very good, Julia," she whispered.

In the darkness, she heard Julia laugh. "And you, my reserved and proper sister, are very, very bad.'' More laughter followed, not without an undertone of malice, and then, after some minutes, Cassandra heard the soft sound of rhythmic breathing that told her Julia was asleep.

Awake in the stillness of the dark chamber, Cassandra thought back to the events of the night—or rather, she thought back to one particular event: Lord Marcheek's kiss. Never had she suspected that a kiss could shake her so, especially a kiss from Lord Marcheek. Although his appearance was attractive enough, she supposed, he did not strike her as anything out of the way. Indeed, his cousin, Mr. Bradford, possessed a much more pleasing air and figure. What little she had seen of Lord Marcheek indicated that he was not a man she would ordinarily wish to kiss. Yet, in spite of her indifference to his charms, not to mention her disapproval of his reputed character, she had been overcome by the press of his lips. His fervour, far from disgusting her, had unleashed hers. Never, except in her paintings of Marietta, had she experienced such powerful emotion. It pained her to think how eager she had been to return the kiss of a man she distrusted and scorned.

Happily, though, she would not be obliged to do more than maintain the barest civility towards Lord Marcheek henceforth. Her promises to Julia ensured that she would be safe from his lordship's impetuosity. She would do everything in her power

to deserve her sister's forgiveness. It ought to be
no great sacrifice to rebuff any attentions such a
man as his lordship might pay her. All she had to
do was remember her duty. Even though the recollection of his touch sent a thrill through her, even
though she could not close her eyes without seeing
his eyes staring intently at her through the white
satin mask, even though she had long dreamed of
meeting the man who would evoke her passion, she
knew precisely what she was obliged to do—for
Julia, for her family, for herself—and she was determined to do it. Any regrets that lingered would,
she devoutly hoped, diminish with time. Near
dawn, with tears still wet on her cheeks, she fell
asleep.

Chapter Six

A Birthday

Cassandra felt relieved, when she and Julia returned from shopping in the village the next day, to learn that the gentlemen of Cantywell had called while they were out. She glanced at their cards, which had been left on a salver in the entrance-hall, and wondered how long she might contrive to avoid their company and all the awkwardness it must excite. Not only was she sensible of her own dread of such a meeting; she felt Julia's, as well. Although it was fitting that her sister's baseless hopes in regard to Lord Marcheek be checked, she ached for her in what must be a time of sorrow and disappointment.

The gentlemen could not be avoided indefinitely, however. Before the week was out, the Vickery sisters found themselves required to meet

Lord Marcheek again. Mr. and Mrs. Bumpers, Ned's fond parents, gave a dinner in honour of their son's birthday and invited all the best families of the neighbourhood. Though their style was not opulent, it was generous. They provided a table laden with boiled leg of mutton, rice pudding, apple dumpling, scalloped oysters, boiled eggs, roasted partridge, jams, molded jellies, blancmange and gooseberry tarts. After admiring this gorgeous banquet, Cassandra was startled to look up and find Lord Marcheek sitting opposite her and, at his right elbow, none other than her sister.

What perverse luck, she thought. The knowledge that Julia must be made uneasy throughout the meal blighted her pleasure in the evening. Even more perverse was the fact that her own dinner partners consisted of Ned Bumpers, who either conversed or ate, never both at once, and the Marquess of Cantywell, who was seized with an attack of biliousness and was determined to quell it with quantities of food and wine. Mr. Bradford, Cassandra noted, was seated far from her at the top of the table by their hostess.

Poor Julia, Cassandra thought again. How would she contrive to say and do all that politeness required of her, seated as she was in such proximity to the man who had exploded her fondest ambitions? With such gloomy musings did she entertain herself through half the courses until she noticed that Julia laughed with excessive mirth at a joke of Lord Marcheek's and in such a manner as to arouse suspicion that far from being angry with the gentleman, she was flirting with him. She looked at him teasingly under heavy lashes and wished only for those dishes which were placed at his elbow and required either his carving or his serving.

Marcheek said, in a voice loud enough for everybody to hear, "I am dashed fond of dining promiscuously. Nobody separates the sexes any more at table, you know, and I for one enjoy my dinner a dashed sight more in consequence." Here he levelled a grin at Julia, which she returned full force.

"Yes," Julia agreed with no evident consciousness of any awkwardness between them. "A formal taking-in is excessively constraining. It is so much more pleasant to be able to sit where one likes." She treated him to a coquettish smile.

Cassandra was incredulous at Julia's conduct. Not a little of her wonder was provoked by the knowledge that she herself had thrown her arms around the neck of this man and kissed him with a passion that would have shocked her parents. She was recalled from these mortifying thoughts when Julia asked Marcheek to tell her of all the current fashions in London.

"We have no way of knowing what is all the crack," Miss Vickery complained. "We are excessively provincial, I fear."

Marcheek obliged with a summary of the new delights that were to be found in Bond Street, following which, Julia cried, ''Oh, how I wish I might see London!''

''Well, I am dashed!'' Marcheek exclaimed. ''Never seen London? I did not think such an unfortunate creature existed.''

''Cassie has seen it, but I have not,'' Julia said, pouting.

''Ah, you have had the pleasure of visiting the most amusing city in the world,'' Marcheek said unctuously to Cassandra.

''I have been required to visit the dentist there,'' Cassandra answered. ''But I, too, would give much to be able to see its sights.''

''Well, you must both see London,'' Marcheek pronounced. ''You must go to a play at Covent Garden and ride the scull to the Tower.''

''Oh, yes, I long to see the Crown Jewels,'' Julia said.

''You must see Hampstead and St. James's, Piccadilly and Madame Tussaud's.''

Julia cried, ''I should like it above anything.''

Cassandra would have added her wishes to the conversation, for she too longed to see the glories of Town, but her thoughts were riveted on what was passing before her. Julia seemed as intent as ever on fixing Lord Marcheek's interest. As to his lordship, she would not have been the least surprised if he were to arrange another secret meeting with Julia so that he might have the kiss he had been cheated of in the library at Cantywell. At this thought, vexation, fear and envy filled Cassandra's head in turn and made her cheeks hot.

"Well, when you do come to Town," said his lordship, "I shall show you all the sights myself. You may depend upon me to put myself entirely at your disposal."

While Julia repaid him with an outpouring of thanks, Cassandra blushed for her sister. It was incredible to her that a girl from such a family as theirs could behave so recklessly. She whispered to Ned, "Do you hear what is passing between Julia and Lord Marcheek?"

Because he had been on the point of attacking a dish in sauce, he replied that he had not been paying them any mind.

"I am afraid that Julia has no more care for her reputation than his lordship does."

Nodding, he said, "Have you tasted the mutton? It is a boiled leg and not at all underdone. I cannot abide a leg that is underdone. I believe I will have just one more spoonful of savoury sauce, if you please."

"I fear his lordship will break Julia's heart, or perhaps even worse," Cassandra said, passing him the sauce.

Clucking, he submerged his mutton in the dark liquid.

In desperation, Cassandra turned to the marquess. "My lord," she said, "is your nephew in the habit of showing visitors about Town? I should think continual engagements prevented his being at the disposal of strangers."

"Oh, he is a most hospitable lad," the marquess replied happily. "I only wish he were not so forgetful, for there have been those—myself included—who, after receiving his particular invitation, have appeared at his door only to find that he had gone to his lodge in Scotland or to Brighton or some such place as that. Most unfortunate, but it is no wonder, for he is prodigiously sought after."

"I can see that he is prodigiously sought after," she replied, glancing at Julia.

Having heard nothing to reassure her that Lord Marcheek was either sincere or steady, Cassandra despaired for her sister. Even more, she despaired for herself as she recalled, for the hundreth time, that the kiss of that same insincere, unsteady gentleman had made her forget herself completely.

After the cover was removed, the dessert and wine were brought in, and as Marcheek and Julia availed themselves of strawberies, raisins and nuts, they gave Cassandra any reassurance she might have lacked that their flirtation continued unabated.

She could understand Lord Marcheek's behaviour—in the library at Cantywell he had promised merely to avoid meeting Julia that evening; nothing had been said of subsequent evenings. Given his reputation, Cassandra was not surprised to find his upright conduct had been unable to outlast a night. But as to Julia, she was mystified. After their intimate conversation the week before, she had expected entirely different conduct from her sister.

She had no opportunity of questioning her until the ladies withdrew, leaving the gentlemen to their bottles and cigar smoke. In the drawing-room, she followed her from the coffee urn to say, "I do not understand, Julia. I believed you intended to do everything in your power to avoid Lord Marcheek. And yet tonight you encouraged the most particular attentions from him."

Julia faced her sister with a smile, and between sips of coffee, explained, "It was not *I* who was to avoid his lordship, if you recall. It was *you*."

"I believed we both wished to avoid him."

"You promised to avoid him, and I agreed that you ought to do so. But I never said I wished to do likewise." A glint of insolence in her eye unsettled Cassandra.

"Then you mean to pursue him, just as before?"

"I see no reason why I should give over all hope of being Lady Marcheek, now that you have promised not to interfere."

"That is not at all what I promised."

"You promised not to stand in my way."

"Oh, Julia, you have deliberately misunderstood my intention."

"Nevertheless, I shall expect you to keep your word."

"But do you know what you are about? You cannot love Lord Marcheek. You scarcely know him, and I am certain you do not know much good of him, except perhaps for his title and his wealth."

Julia smiled. "These are no small considerations to me, even if they are to you. But I must allow, Cassie, I have an even greater cause for finding him perfectly charming, namely, your interference. It has given a spur to my resolve. Nothing is quite so amusing as triumphing over a rival."

"I see. You pursue him out of spite, then?"

"To a degree, a very large degree. But his lordship is possessed of many other charms, as well, the principal one being his house in Town."

"And you would sacrifice reputation, love, happiness—everything, in short—because a gentleman has a house in Town?"

"I do not expect you to comprehend a creature of my sensibility; you are too lacking in spirit. But I have been suffocated all my life, and if I do not leave this place and go to London, I shall go distracted!"

Cassandra closed her eyes as it came to her that until now, she had not understood her sister in the least.

Mr. Bradford had glanced Cassandra's way so often during dinner that Mrs. Bumpers had remarked upon it. After that, he had been careful to keep his eyes on his hostess, though his thoughts continued to wander towards that part of the table where the young lady sat. He guessed that the Misses Vickery were deliberately avoiding him and his cousin, and after what had transpired at the ball, he could not be surprised, but he could be— and was—dissatisfied with such a state of affairs. The kiss in the library leapt to mind frequently, and at the most inopportune moments. He could not help wishing to speak to the young woman with whom he had shared it. Perhaps he might improve her estimation of him. Perhaps the improvement would be so great that he might one day tell her who in fact had kissed her in the library. Perhaps by the time he did tell her, she would have forgotten all about Marcheek.

Upon entering the drawing-room with the other gentlemen, he looked for Cassandra and, seeing her seated quite alone on a sofa, approached. "Good evening," he said with a bow. On her invitation, he took the seat next to her on the sofa. "I had begun to think I should never have another opportunity of bidding you good-evening. It has been some time since we have met. One would almost think you wished to avoid my company.'' He knew he had hit on the truth, for she coloured.

''Oh, but we met at the ball,'' she said breathlessly.

''Ah, you do not consider a week a very long time to be apart from one's friends?'' He smiled at her and was gratified to see her return his smile.

A pause ensued, during which they continued to smile, giving Mr. Bradford the hope that he might now speak candidly. He had not forgotten his vow to speak to Miss Cassandra in regard to her art and had thought long about the best means of broaching the subject. He knew that she did not quite trust him, and now that he had lied to her in two momentous instances, he could not blame her. Still, he felt obliged to exhort her not to throw away her talent, and he believed that at this moment, while she was smiling at him, he must seize his opportunity. Preparing to begin his speech, he leaned towards her, but she spoke first.

Looking directly at him with earnest eyes, she said, ''Mr. Bradford, how is it that members of the same family can be so utterly different from each other? I fail to comprehend it.''

''You allude, no doubt, to my cousin and myself,'' he said, amused at this sudden turn of the topic. ''Yes, Marcheek and I do differ in many aspects. In figure and countenance, of course, there is a resemblance—the Cantywell nose, the square chin, the brown eyes.''

''I was not speaking merely of appearances.''

''You were speaking of character, I collect. I expect Marcheek and I do differ somewhat there. I am thought serious, too serious by half, some would have it, while he, on the other hand, has never in his life been mistaken for a serious fellow.''

''It is no wonder that you are different, even opposite in some points, for you were raised in different households. But how is it that two creatures—sisters, for example—can live all their lives in the same house, guided by the same parents and the same principles, and still turn out so unlike?''

Mr. Bradford guessed at once which two sisters Cassandra alluded to. Swiftly, he scanned the room and found Julia sitting in a corner—with Marcheek. The heated glances with which she favoured him enlightened Mr. Bradford as to the cause of Cassandra's anxiety. He felt a surge of anger at Marcheek, who was apparently heading for the same rabbit trap he had been at such pains to avoid the night of the Cantywell ball. And he felt a surge of something else as he wondered if Miss Cassandra's concern for her sister concealed more than a tinge of jealousy.

All at once, he saw the two of them set their

coffee cups on a table and slip out the door. Julia giggled conspiratorially as they went. Immediately, Mr. Bradford looked at Cassandra to ascertain whether she, too, had seen the sudden departure. One glimpse at her pained expression told him that she had. When her eyes met his, he found himself arrested by her genuine alarm. He would not have been surprised if she had burst into tears.

To his amusement, she gave an excellent imitation of a shrug and said, with exaggerated unconcern, "Do not look at me so, Mr. Bradford. I take no notice of what we have just witnessed. The imprudence of others is nothing to me. I have made a vow to interfere no more."

Smiling, he congratulated her on her resolution. "You are remarkably wise, for I have observed that one is never thanked for interfering, no matter how selfless and worthy the motive. Whenever I have interfered on my cousin's behalf, I have been repaid with ungrateful reproaches. I shall not make the same mistake again."

"Nor shall I. It is useless to meddle, especially when others are resolved upon ruining themselves forever."

"I believe it was a great sage who observed that only a fool is so unwise as to meddle in another's concerns."

He was prepared to hear her continue in the same vein, but abruptly she put a hand to her forehead and stood. He saw her inhale, as if to summon her courage. "Mr. Bradford," she said, "I must ask a favour of you."

He rose, saying, "I am flattered that you trust me so far as to allow me to perform a service."

"Will you tell your cousin, in the most discreet manner you can contrive, that I wish to meet with him?"

"What?" In this instance, he was not at all amused at the sudden turn of the subject.

"I must speak with him. I must ask him once again to have a care for my sister's reputation."

"But did you not speak with him on that very point at the ball?"

"Yes, upon your kind recommendation I spoke with him in the library, and he obliged me then. I am hoping he will oblige me again."

"I do not see that he is very obliging if you must go to him every week with the same request."

"When we met, we spoke only of his appointment with Julia in the library. Now I wish to speak with him of his conduct in general towards my sister."

"Let me entreat you, Miss Cassandra, to allow me to speak to him for you. Where the ladies are concerned, my cousin is not always to be trusted."

"What do you mean?"

"I think you know very well what I mean." He felt her studying him closely.

At last, she moistened her lips and asked, "Did Lord Marcheek tell you what passed between us in the library at Cantywell?"

He considered carefully before replying, "I can say in all truthfulness that Lord Marcheek and I have not exchanged a single syllable on the subject."

Her relief was evident. "Your cousin has been discreet. I confess, I did not expect it of him."

"I shall be happy to say to him whatever you wish me to say."

"Thank you, but I am afraid I must speak with him myself."

"Must you, indeed? And why is that?"

He saw her turn a fiery shade of pink. With an effort, she replied, "In addition to the matter of my sister, there is another matter between us which was left unsettled. I wish to settle it, once and for all."

It occurred to him that she was alluding to the kiss, and he could not help wondering how she meant to settle the matter. Curious though he was, however, he could not allow her to meet with Marcheek. His cousin would be sure to blab that it was not he who had worn the mask of white satin but his cousin James. Worse, Marcheek might avail himself of the opportunity to fix himself in Cassandra's good graces. Sternly, he said, "Did we not just agree that it is folly to interfere in the business of others?''

She lowered her eyes. ''Yes, we did.''

''And is not this meeting you wish to have with my cousin for the very purpose of interfering?''

Ruefully, she nodded. ''Yes, it is.''

''But you are resolved on this course nonetheless?''

''If your intention is to point out to me my hypocrisy, please do not put yourself to the trouble. I am well aware of it. Will you assist me, or must I ask your cousin myself?''

He could not forbear smiling. For a quiet, prim young lady, Miss Cassandra Vickery certainly could be bold—but bold in a manner that appealed to him. She was intrepid without being impertinent, daring without being brazen. In that respect, she resembled her paintings. Even her pitiful daisy had a quality of directness he very much admired.

''I have no intention of pointing out your hypocrisy or anyone else's,'' he assured her. ''I merely wish to be certain we understand each other, for, you see, I intend to interfere, as well.''

''You do?''

''My dear Miss Cassandra, do you think you are the only one here who is determined to commit folly? I assure you, I am as foolish and contradictory as anybody in this room. And I mean to prove it, for as soon as I take leave of you, I shall go after my cousin and give him the throttling of his life.''

Laughing, she enquired, ''And will you kindly pause in your throttling just long enough to inform his lordship that I wish to meet with him?''

He assured her that he would. ''Naturally, you wish to meet with him in secret.''

''Oh, yes. No one must know of this, especially not Julia.''

''At the stroke of midnight, I suppose.''

''That will do well enough.''

''I thought as much. When and where is this meeting to take place?''

''I do not know. Perhaps I shall leave that to him.''

''I shall bring you his answer tomorrow.''

''I shall stay at home till you come.''

His eyes rested on her for a time, and then recollecting where he was and what he had just promised to do, he said, ''Until tomorrow, then,'' and bowed himself off.

Cassandra felt great pity for Ned Bumpers. In the excitement of approaching her, he bobbed his head furiously. She would not have been surprised to hear him give out with a cock-a-doodle-doo. ''What is it, Mr. Bumpers?'' she asked soothingly. ''Is there something you wish to say to me?''

"Oh, indeed there is, Miss Cassandra. It is the most splendid thing. It is my birthday, you know."

"I do know, and though I have already extended to you my warmest felicitations, permit me to do so again."

"No, no, you do not understand. My birthday is not in the least splendid."

"I do not know how you can say so. I am sure your parents have given you a most festive party. If such a grand dinner were given in my honour, I should consider it very splendid, indeed."

"Oh, dear, you are angry with me. I cannot abide it when anyone is angry with me."

"I promise you, I am not angry with you—unless, that is, you intend to be ungrateful to your parents for this excellent party."

"Ungrateful is the last thing I am, I assure you. I am the most grateful creature on Earth. You see, my mother and father have given me the most splendid birthday gift. They have taken a house in Bath for the Season. Is that not splendid?"

"Yes, it is, given that your mother and father are devoted to the country and speak of life anywhere else with the profoundest distaste."

"Exactly what I thought myself." His chin thrust in her direction three times in rapid succession. "But they have concluded it is their duty to take me where there is diverse society and where

I may be dressed in the finest style and meet young people of refinement and fashion.''

With heartfelt good will, she wished him pleasure in the anticipated adventure.

''I mean to like Bath prodigiously, but I do not think I shall like leaving my acquaintance.''

''You will form new acquaintance,'' she reassured him.

''Yes, but they may not like me as well as my acquaintance in Hopcross. You may not think so, Miss Cassandra, but there have been those who have regarded me as a bumpkin. I should not like to be laughed at in Bath.''

''Those who know how good-hearted you are will not laugh.''

This response pleased him. Looking significantly at her, he said, ''Still, there are one or two friends I shall miss prodigiously.''

''And they shall miss you, too, I am sure.''

At this, he held his head perfectly still. ''Do you think so?''

''Why, yes. I should not say so otherwise.''

With his breath coming quickly, he begged, ''Miss Cassandra, may I presume to pay you a visit soon?''

''Mr. Bumpers, as you have been a fixture at the rectory these many years, I cannot think why you should have any doubt of your welcome now.''

He would have replied with all the ardour at his

command, but her attention was summoned by the opening of the door. Julia entered, wearing red cheeks and her customary pout. Lord Marcheek was not to be seen anywhere. In his place was Mr. Bradford, upon whose arm her sister leaned heavily. For the remainder of the evening, Mr. Bradford kept to Julia's side. Nowhere was Lord Marcheek to be seen. In fact, he did not appear at all that night, a fact which rendered Cassandra acutely uneasy. She scolded herself for hoping to catch sight of him in spite of everything she knew to his detriment. Ever since she had left the schoolroom and become a young lady of independent mind and opinion, she had scorned those heroines of the stage and the lending library who allowed themselves to fall in love with knaves and villains. She had never been able to understand how women of sense could behave so imprudently. However, she was beginning to understand. Her preoccupation with the man in the mask of white satin was as powerful as ever and gave no promise of abating.

Chapter Seven

The Meeting Is Arranged

The sisters retired for the night and awoke the next morning without exchanging a word. Cassandra kept silent because she feared she might inadvertently let slip her plan to speak with Lord Marcheek. Julia was too absorbed in her own concerns to make the effort of conversation. Indeed, it seemed to Cassandra that she scarcely noticed the existence of any other human creature, until they were seated in the parlour with Ned Bumpers, who had come to call.

Mrs. Vickery said, "You have my congratulations, Mr. Bumpers. I understand you are soon to make a journey of some distance from Hopcross."

At that moment, Cassandra observed, her sister suddenly recovered from her fit of the sullens.

"You intend to travel, Mr. Bumpers?" Julia enquired with uncharacteristic cordiality.

"Oh, yes. My father has let a house in Bath."

"Oh, you are only going to Bath," she murmured, let down.

Taking umbrage at her tone, he said, "You cannot have any objection to Bath, Miss Vickery. To my knowledge, you have never been there."

She replied loftily, "If your father was going to all the trouble of letting a house, I wonder that he did not take one in Town."

Ned's head fluttered as he said, "My father says he does not know a more uncivil place than Town."

Julia rose heatedly to the defence of the capital. "I daresay, if one cannot find civility in London, it is not to be found anywhere. It is London which sets the manners and style of the entire world."

Affronted at this reflection on his sire's taste, Ned retorted, "If my father thinks London uncivil, Miss Vickery, I am certain he has good reason. Papa is never wrong."

Before Julia could reply with equal energy, Cassandra said, "Perhaps Mr. Bumpers's father dislikes the noise and traffic of the Town. Perhaps he regards a house in Bath as a situation more conducive to excellent health in addition to excellent society."

Julia was not to be distracted. "Bath is not fashionable any longer. The ton do not frequent it if they can help it. The whole world knows that one does better to go to Brighton than to Bath.''

''Oh,'' said Ned, wounded.

''Are there camels in Bath?'' one of the young children asked.

''I don't expect there are,'' Ned said.

''Mr. Bradford rode an elephant in India,'' chimed in one of the boys. ''Will you ride an elephant in Bath?''

''I expect there are no elephants,'' answered Ned miserably.

''I suppose there are no tigers, either,'' the littlest girl said scornfully.

Utterly deflated, he shook his head and mourned, ''I do not think I shall like Bath very well, after all.''

''For myself,'' said the rector, sipping his tea. ''I always think that home is best. What is the use of flying thither and yon when everything one wants is right at hand? I never go beyond Hopcross unless compelled to.'' Contentedly, he tousled the heads of the children at his feet and ate his cake with smacking relish, while Julia levelled at him a look of the profoundest woe.

The family and their guest sat in silence for some minutes until Mr. Bradford was announced. At the sound of the name, Julia came to attention. Then, seeing that the gentleman was unaccompanied, she receded into her petulance. Cassandra, too, had grown alert at the sound of the name. The smile he gave her told her that, as promised, he had brought an answer to her message.

After thanking Mr. Bradford for honouring her poor parlour with his presence, Mrs. Vickery offered him a chair and a cup of tea along with the information that Mr. Bumpers was to go to Bath in the fall.

"Do you go to take the waters?" Mr. Bradford enquired.

"My parents wish me to go, and so I suppose I must."

"Mr. Bumpers has never before been to Bath," Cassandra said.

"Well, then," Mr. Bradford replied amiably, "if you visit the Pump Room, as everybody must in Bath, you must be sure to taste a cup of the waters."

"Oh, have you visited Bath?" Ned asked hopefully. "Have you tasted the waters? Did you like them?"

"Nobody likes them, I'm afraid, but one ought to have a taste of them if one visits Bath. One's health may not improve, but I am certain one's character is strengthened by having to drink anything so vile."

"I do not see why my parents wish to take me to a place as unfashionable and disagreeable as Bath," Ned mourned. "I am sure I shall not like it at all.'' On that, he bade farewell to his hosts and took his leave, his head bobbing dejectedly.

''Mr. Bumpers has an aversion to Bath, I collect,'' said Mr. Bradford.

''There are no camels or elephants,'' offered one of the children. ''Nor any tigers, neither.''

''Well, that accounts for it,'' Mr. Bradford replied, smiling.

After ten minutes, during which he enchanted the Vickerys with the story of his sighting of a whale in the North Sea, the tea was removed, the children were herded to the schoolroom and the gentleman found himself alone with Cassandra. She sat at a small writing table by an open window through which a summer breeze blew. It was a delightful picture, he thought: a young lady of uncommon grace set against a background of shrubbery and hazy blue sky, all of it framed by the window. The picture appealed to him as a collector, and as a man.

He rose from his chair to place a small folded parchment before her on the table. The wax seal bore Lord Marcheek's crest. She looked up at Mr. Bradford, swallowed and opened the paper. A moment later, she folded it again and thanked him.

''Are you certain you do not wish to change your mind?'' he asked kindly. ''I am still yours to command, if you wish.''

She sighed. His solicitude brought home to her,

not for the first time, the irony, not to mention the impropriety, of her plan. Not only was she about to risk her reputation as dangerously as she had feared her sister might, but she was doing it with the full consciousness that she was to meet a man who was not to be trusted with the ladies, a man who had kissed her, and moreover, whom she had kissed in return.

Her motive for meeting this gentleman, she had told herself, was to rescue Julia. Seeing Mr. Bradford's expression of concern, however, she felt a flush of shame. Was that indeed her motive, she asked herself. Was she perhaps secretly anxious to meet again with the gentleman who had kissed her? Was she perhaps as desperate for adventure as Julia? Was she perhaps as eager to rush headlong into scandal and ruination to find it? Was she even more wicked than Julia because she had promised faithfully that she would not so much as speak to Marcheek and was now going back on her word?

Ashamed, Cassandra began to think better of her plan to meet his lordship in secret. Instead, she reflected, she ought to place her trust in Mr. Bradford. She ought to put Lord Marcheek's kiss entirely out of her thoughts. It had been, after all, merely the kiss of a rake. If she had a groat's worth of sense, she would turn her back on such a man and accept the assistance of his cousin, who, she had come to see, was well mannered, gentle, patient, astute, worldly and anxious to be of service to her.

Taking a breath, she looked up at him, smiled and mustered her courage to speak, but before she could utter a sound, he leaned across the table so that his face came close to hers and said, ''If I cannot persuade you to give up this notion of meeting my cousin, may I at least entreat you not to give up your art?''

Instinctively, she drew back and gazed at him as though he had struck her. ''I beg your pardon?''

''Some time ago, you told me you intended to give up your art forever. I have been meaning to speak to you about it ever since, but have been prevented until now. I am obliged to tell you, as somewhat of a collector and, I fancy, an authority, I think that is a grave mistake, one you will regret.''

Cassandra was certain that he had seen her pictures. Why else would he take it upon himself to interfere so officiously in her most private concerns? Angrily, she stood. ''Mr. Bradford, whether I choose to continue drawing daisies or not is no affair of yours!''

He rose as well and smiled. ''We have agreed, have we not, that it is folly to interfere in matters that do not concern us? We have also agreed that we feel compelled to interfere nonetheless. Hence, though your daisies are, as you say, no affair of mine, I choose to make them my affair by urging you not to renounce them.''

In a swift motion, she moved past him on her way to the door. He caught her by the arm.

''Let me go,'' she said, barely containing her outrage.

Seeing the emotion on her face, he removed his hand. Slowly, reluctantly, he stepped back. ''It was not my intention to offend,'' he said as tranquilly as his own emotion would allow. ''Indeed, I meant to encourage. I do not understand why you are determined to be affronted by what is intended as praise.''

''And I do not understand why you persist in praising my daisy when you know perfectly well it is dreadful. You do not mean to encourage me, Mr. Bradford. You mean to scoff at me.''

''Perhaps *you* are the one who scoffs, Miss Cassandra. It seems to me that I esteem your artistic endeavours more highly than you do.''

Suppressing the stinging retorts that leapt to her tongue, she collected herself sufficiently to say, ''I shall be obliged if you will inform his lordship that I will meet him at the appointed time.'' On that, she hurried into the entrance and bade the maidservant show Mr. Bradford the door.

As soon as he returned to Cantywell, Mr. Bradford met his cousin, whom he found in the garden, carrying a glass and a decanter of brandy and inspecting an artfully arranged circle of sweet william and lupins.

"There you are, James," his lordship greeted him. "I have been waiting a dashed long time to tell you what I've uncovered."

"It had better not be female, Marcheek. I am in too foul a mood for one of your females. Or any female, for that matter."

After studying his cousin's grim face, Marcheek poured out a glass and handed it to him.

Mr. Bradford glared briefly at the grin of the giver and availed himself of the drink.

"There, that is better," the young lord observed after Mr. Bradford had finished the draught. "And the news I have will set you up in even finer fettle. What do you think, James? I have found out a gaming-house. I intend to grace its tables tomorrow evening."

Mr. Bradford grimaced and took another drink. "I suppose it was too much to hope that you had decided to take holy orders."

"It is only an hour's ride. We may stay overnight at The Star and Garter. Dash it, how is it possible to be dull at an inn named The Star and Garter? It will be a merry night, of which we have not seen the likes in too dashed long a time. We shall start out directly after tea."

''I thank you, but I must decline. I am appointed to meet a lady.''

''You are bamming me, James. You are not the sort who meets ladies. The truth is, you have a picture you mean to squint at, or you feel obliged to sit up with my uncle smoking a pipe and digesting your dinner.''

''No, I am to meet a lady, though I heartily wish I were not.''

''Well, then, permit me to turn the tables on you, coz, and treat you to the advice you recently gave me, to wit, do not keep the appointment. Accompany me instead.''

''Tell me, Marcheek. Do you really mean to visit a gaming-house, or do you plan to meet a lady yourself?''

Incensed, Marcheek demanded, ''Do you impugn my integrity? When have you ever known me to fail to keep my promise to visit a gaming-house?''

Mr. Bradford smiled. ''Never. You have been entirely faithful in that regard. I merely thought that as you have revived your flirtation with Miss Vickery, you might have been persuaded to meet her again.''

On this, Marcheek seized the glass and took it away from Mr Bradford, cradling it indignantly to his bosom. ''I am grieved, deeply grieved, by this accusation,'' he sniffed. ''What do you take me for, a dunce? You have made it abundantly clear that if I meet with this damsel, lovely though she is, I shall in all likelihood end up shackled to a wife before my time. You do not need to warn me above a dozen times, you know. I have learnt that I am safer in a gaming-house than in Miss Vickery's clutches, and, in truth, the same may be said of you. If you keep your appointment tonight, you may be the one to end up shackled.''

Mr. Bradford laughed ruefully. ''It is always easier to give advice than to heed it.''

''Well, as a rule, I do neither. However, in this case, I have done as you advise, and though I did slip away from the party with Miss Vickery last night, it was at her instigation. I abandoned her at once in the hall.''

''So she informed me.''

''I daresay, she was in a dashed snit.''

''She was very angry with you, but I do not think she intends to give up the pursuit merely on account of your rudeness.''

''She will give it up in time. I am much more adept at evading pursuers than she is at pursuing.''

''I have your word, then? You will not attempt to attach Miss Vickery's heart?''

''You have my word. But I must caution you, James. She may love me all the better for my indifference. It happens frequently. The more I dislike a lady, the more she is resolved to have me.''

"Ah, so indifference is the secret, is it?" Mr. Bradford mused. "I had thought that one went about winning a fair lady's heart by being earnest, sincere, devoted and kind."

Shaking his head in exasperation, Marcheek said, "I'm dashed if I know where you acquire such outlandish ideas, James. Clearly, you have spent far too much time out of England. You could not possibly have heard such absurdity at home."

On leaving his cousin, Mr. Bradford scoured the house for Mrs. Clapshew, the housekeeper, a female of generous proportions and mighty opinions. He found her in the kitchen garden, gathering lettuces for the marquess's salad. It was the joy of Mrs. Clapshew's life to do whatever pleased the marquess, whom she had served with zeal for more than half a century.

"A word with you, Mrs. Clapshew, if you please," said Mr. Bradford, raising his hat.

She beamed a smile on her master's nephew and invited him to join her in touring the rows of greens and cucumbers. "What may I do for you, sir?" she asked.

"I was wondering whether you were engaged tomorrow, in the evening—at midnight, to be precise."

She eyed him suspiciously, then stopped to turn a cucumber over. Finding it yellow on the underside, she left it to ripen on the vine, saying, "I believe I shall be engaged in sleeping in my bed, as any woman my age ought to be at such an hour."

"Quite right, Mrs. Clapshew. I only thought you might be at liberty to assist Miss Cassandra Vickery."

"Miss Cassandra—the rector's daughter?"

"The very same. I believe you are acquainted with her."

"Acquainted with her? Why, I assisted the midwife at her birth. I sewed her sleeping gowns. I brought her nurse the balm for her teething. I dandled her on my knee and warned her of all the snares little girls must beware."

"Perhaps you are fond of her, Mrs. Clapshew."

"Only her mother is fonder of her than I. A sweeter, more sensible, modest child I have never known. She does not put herself forward or puff herself up as her sister does. She is what you will not often meet with in this age of vice."

"Hearing your encomiums on her, I am emboldened to ask whether you would be so kind as to act as her chaperon when I meet her tomorrow night?"

The housekeeper nearly stepped on a row of radish in her shock. "Mr. Bradford! Do you intend to ruin the poor girl?"

"Not at all."

"Your meeting with her in secret will do nothing to prevent it, I can assure you. In point of fact, it will promote it."

"If we do not tell anyone of the meeting, I am confident no scandal will result."

"I am as closed-mouthed as anybody, but apart from the scandal of the thing, it is wrong, Mr. Bradford, very wrong. I beg you not to do this."

"It must be done."

"If so, then it is because you are as bad as your cousin. You are a pair, the two of you, thinking only of yourselves, never considering what might please your uncle or ruin a fine young lady's hopes forever."

"Permit me to ask you a question, Mrs. Clapshew."

"A question! A question! You are proposing the seduction of a child who has been like a daughter to me, and you presume to ask a question, as though we were bargaining over a bushel of parsnips. I had thought better of you than that, Mr. Bradford. I had thought you had more sense than that rapscallion of a young lord you call cousin and would never stoop to do a young lady a rascally turn."

Mr. Bradford waited patiently as she continued her tirade.

"Moreover, sir, if you wish to inform my master that I have spoken my mind to you without disguise, if you wish to say that I have overstepped the bounds of a servant, then by all means do so. I do not apologize for speaking the truth pure and simple to a scamp half my age, but will just go and pack my valises and bid goodbye to the only home I have known these fifty years.'' She paused for breath long enough to wipe away a tear.

Mr. Bradford handed her his linen, and when she had blown her nose, he said pleasantly, ''My question is this: if I proposed to seduce Miss Cassandra, would I have invited you to act as her chaperon?''

She peered at him over the linen, her eyes narrowing as she considered this logic.

''What do you propose, then, if I may be so bold, sir?''

''It is a private matter which concerns Miss Julia Vickery and Lord Marcheek.''

''I see. But why must you meet in secret, and at night?''

''Miss Cassandra thinks it best, and because she is, as you say, the sweetest, most modest and sensible young lady in the world, I have agreed. But I did think it wise to invite a chaperon along, and I could think of no one better suited than yourself to protect the young lady, though I assure you, she will not require protection from me.''

Scowling, Mrs. Clapshew inspected the linen. ''I shall have this laundered before your meeting tomorrow night.''

"Then you agree?"

"I expect someone had better be at the ready, and it may as well be me."

"I heartily thank you."

"I do not do it for your sake, sir, but for Miss Cassandra's. I mean to look out for her welfare."

She also meant to look out for the means of making a match between Mr. Bradford and Cassandra. Although the gentleman was as impertinent as a puppy, he was amazingly rich and quite handsome, and, unlike his cousin, she saw, he was capable of behaving like a man of honour, as evidenced by his asking her to act as chaperon. Nothing would give her greater pleasure than to see her dear Cassandra well married to a future baronet.

Of course, Mrs. Clapshew had no intention of giving him the satisfaction of telling him so. Indeed, Mrs. Clapshew considered it entirely unnecessary to burden Mr. Bradford with any of these reflections. And lest he see how much she had softened towards him, she scowled at him and rolled her eyes for good measure.

"I mean to look out for her welfare, too," he said, and planted a kiss on her cheek.

"Humph," she replied, turning crimson.

"Until then." He bestowed on her a most respectful bow.

"Tomorrow night," she muttered.

"At midnight. And by the by," he said as he left her, "do not be alarmed if the young lady addresses me as Lord Marcheek and I appear wearing a mask of white satin."

Mrs. Clapshew dropped her jaw and her basket, but it was too late to protest. He was gone.

Chapter Eight

A Sack of Flour

Early on the fateful day, Cassandra ransacked her mind for a way of slipping from the house that night without waking Julia. Because her sister was not a sound sleeper, the likelihood was small that her plan to meet Marcheek would go undiscovered. As morning turned to afternoon it seemed prudent to give up the plan altogether, either by sending word by way of Mr. Bradford or by sending it in her own handwriting, both of which she was loath to do. The only alternative, she concluded at last, was to send no word at all, but simply fail to appear at the appointed hour. Her cheeks flamed when she imagined in what capricious and untrustworthy light she must appear to Lord Marcheek as he waited for her minute after minute, perhaps hour after hour, to no avail. She could only hope that Fate would give her an opportunity at some future date to explain herself.

Meanwhile, she consoled herself with painting. Her newest pasteboard portrayed Marietta reclining on a lily-pad which flew over a patchwork of yellow and green fields. A hazy city loomed in the distance. As the delicate sea nymph looked towards her destination, her beribboned curls blew in the breeze and her bare toes peeked from beneath her gown.

Cassandra was sighing over this adventurous water-colour when Julia entered the attic room to inform her that she had been invited to spend a week at Sparrowdene, where Lady Monck and her daughters were so dull as to require company.

Hiding her painting, Cassandra asked, "Have you accepted?"

Julia paused in the hurry of gathering her dresses to eye her with defiance. "And what if I have? What is that to you?"

"Oh, Julia, I hope you do not anticipate meeting Lord Marcheek at Sparrowdene. Lady Monck is not well and entertains rarely, I am told."

"Lady Monck is feeling a good deal better, according to my information, and even if she were not, I should still have a greater opportunity of meeting his lordship at Sparrowdene than I do here, for you thwart me at every turn. I shall write his lordship at the first opportunity and let him know where he may find me. You shall have no further opportunity to deprive me of amusement.''

''It was never my intention, Julia, to deprive you of amusement. I am sorry if you thought it was. I merely wished to see you safe.''

Smiling cunningly, Julia replied, ''Well, now you shall see me not at all, and it is no less than you deserve. I tell you, Cassie, before we are done, you shall have your comeuppance and I shall have my revenge.''

Stung, Cassandra repeated, ''Revenge?''

''When I am Lady Marcheek, you will be very sorry you tried to come between me and his lordship. I shall not frank your correspondence. Nor shall I invite you to Town for the Season.''

Pained at being so misunderstood, Cassandra could make no retort. She watched in silence as Julia, with noisy irritability, collected her things. At last, their mother came in to oversee the remainder of the packing, and when she pronounced it done and the servant had carried off the valises, Julia ran from the chamber without so much as a goodbye to her sister.

There was no avoiding Lord Marcheek now, it seemed, no excuse to fail to keep their rendezvous. It was more critical than ever to keep her sister from harm. Hours hence, at the stroke of midnight, she must do the thing she had pledged to do.

* * *

The sky was bright with moonlight as she walked with much trepidation towards the north edge of the Cantywell estate. Letting herself in at the iron gate, she took the gravel path along a row of oaks until she came to the outskirts of a copse, on the far side of which stood a reproduction of a Greek temple consisting of a rounded platform with four steps, four columns and a dome overhead.

From behind a tree stepped a cloaked figure, startling her. It seized her hand and whispered, "Do not be afraid, my child. It is I, Mrs. Clapshew."

Blushing to be discovered out of doors at such an unseemly hour, Cassandra said, "Oh, dear."

"All is well, Miss Cassandra. The gentleman sent me. I am to be your chaperon."

Cassandra was astonished at this announcement. The last thing she had expected of Lord Marcheek was a mark of courtesy and care. This uncharacteristic gallantry on his part bolstered her confidence, as did the sight of an old acquaintance whom she regarded with deep affection. "This is very kind of you," she said to the housekeeper, "and of Lord Marcheek."

"As to the gentleman, I say nothing for I've promised to keep my own counsel, and I am not one to go back on my word. I said to him it was very wrong to have you meet him in such a manner, but would he listen? No, for he was deaf to all sense. However, you shall have nothing to fear. I shall be on the lookout.''

Tucking her arm through Mrs. Clapshew's, Cassandra allowed herself to be escorted to the temple. Half hidden by a pillar was a dim masculine figure. Though the fragrant night was warm, he wore a cloak and large hat, which gave him the air of a highwayman. Cassandra drew in a breath at the sight of him. Hearing it, Mrs. Clapshew whispered, ''You have only to call out, and I shall be here in a flash.''

After thanking her protector, Cassandra ascended the steps of the temple.

The figure moved to greet her. As a moonbeam caught his face, she stopped stock-still. ''You are masked!'' she said.

''Indeed I am,'' came the reply.

''But why?''

''So that if anybody should come upon us, we shall not be recognized.''

''It is unlikely that anybody will be taking the air at this hour of the night.''

''Dash it, you may be right. On the other hand, if we have designated this place for our rendezvous, why should others not do likewise? Seems a dashed convenient spot for it.''

''Even if you were right and others were to intrude upon our privacy,'' Cassandra argued, ''your being masked will not prevent *my* being discovered.''

''Aha! The very same notion occurred to me. That is why I took the precaution of hunting up the masks your mother was so kind as to return to my uncle.''

Cassandra found herself presented with the peacock-blue mask she had worn to the Cantywell ball. She glanced at the gentleman sceptically.

''Well, put it on,'' he urged.

''I do not not wish to put it on. This is not a game, my lord.''

He laughed. ''Of course it is a game, and a dashed lively one, too.'' On that, he stepped close to her, removed the shawl she wore over her hair and fastened the mask round her head. Stepping back, he admired his work. ''I'm dashed if that is not a dashed romantical sight.''

''I feel ridiculous.''

''Well, the romantical often makes one feel ridiculous. There is a cure for that, however.''

''And I am certain you know what it is.''

''As a matter of fact, I do, and it is this: practise. One must practise being romantical until one has got entirely accustomed to feeling ridiculous.''

''Lord Marcheek, I did not come here under these circumstances to discuss what is romantical.''

''That is a great pity, for it is a dashed fine evening.'' Standing by her side, so that his shoulder brushed hers, he directed her attention to the sky. ''I do not know when I have seen such a splendid display. The stars shine so brightly in the country. There are no gas lamps and traffic to obscure them.''

Cassandra saw that the stars were as plentiful as blossoms on a honeysuckle. ''You are a puzzle, my lord,'' she said.

Turning his eyes from the sky, he looked at her. ''Why am I a puzzle—because I admire the stars on a brilliant night? Surely, a man who enjoys the pleasures of the Town may appreciate those of the rural regions, as well.''

''One moment you are an egregious flirt, and the next you pause to admire the beauty of the heavens. One moment you are so magnanimous as to ask Mrs. Clapshew to act as my chaperon, and the next you speak in the most frivolous manner. You are a perfect contradiction, my lord.''

He drew nearer. ''Is that so surprising? Are you not a contradiction yourself? Do you not pass yourself off in the world as a diffident, reserved young lady, the very model of a rector's daughter, and yet are you not in fact romantical? Did you not meet me alone in the library at Cantywell? And did you not invite me to meet you alone tonight?''

Mortified, she walked to a pillar and frowned.

"A gentleman would not have thrown such inconsistencies in my face."

"I merely wish to illustrate that appearances count for very little. What truly matters is what lies beneath our...our masks, so to speak."

"Very well, you have proved me a hypocrite."

"I do not believe you are a hypocrite. However, you may believe me to be one, for I am not what I appear to be. When I am alone with you, as now, I find it impossible to be the insouciant, foolish fellow I am accustomed to being. If I appear inconsistent, the fault is yours, Miss Cassandra. You affect me as no other woman ever has." He moved a step nearer.

His proximity made her aware of a warm sensation about her neck. She stepped back, doubting that he was as sincere as he sounded but certain that she was in danger of liking him more than was prudent. She cleared her throat. "Sir, I was compelled to meet you tonight for the same reason as before—my sister. I am afraid she is still bent on ruining herself for your sake."

All at once, he seemed to recollect Julia. In a light tone, he said, "Oh, yes, Miss Vickery. A dashed charming girl. I congratulate you on your family."

"Once again, I ask you to have a care for her reputation and her affections."

"Once again, I give you my promise."

"I have come to know you somewhat these past weeks, Lord Marcheek, and it seems to me that you are not without either benevolence or conscience. I appeal to both when I beg you to refrain from giving my sister any false notion that you might be induced to marry her."

"I was under the impression that I had just given you my promise, but I have no objection to repeating it. I take my oath, Miss Cassandra, that I shall so refrain."

"So you promised in the library, but at Monday's dinner you flirted with her in the most thoughtless manner."

"I never contradict a charming young lady, but in this case I cannot do otherwise. It was your sister who flirted with me."

"Sir, you vowed to put yourself at her disposal when she visited London."

"I make the same vow to everyone who threatens to come up to Town. But I never do put myself at their disposal, you know. You may ask my uncle, if you do not believe me."

"You stole out of the drawing-room with my sister, and the two of you were tittering. Do not deny it. I saw you, and so did Mr. Bradford."

"But I do deny it, for although it is true that she plagued me until I was persuaded to leave the safety of the drawing-room, I did not titter. I consider it beneath the dignity of an earl to titter. Fur-

thermore, I was no sooner out the door than I left
her to her own devices and went immediately to
Cantywell. If you do not believe me, ask my cousin
James. He found Miss Vickery alone in the hall
stamping her feet and shaking her fists. He had to
stick by her side the entire evening to calm her, so
great was her fury.''

Distressed, Cassandra said, ''It is not the part of
a gentleman to place all the blame on the lady in
the case, even when the blame does lie entirely
with her.''

He came to her and began to reach for her hand.
Then he checked himself, saying only, ''I am sorry
to be the one to tell you what must give you pain,
but I cannot blind myself to what your sister is. I
can only assure you, again and again if I must, that
nothing will tempt me to take advantage of it.''

Sorrowfully, she shook her head. ''Do not apologize, my lord.'' Looking at him squarely, she confessed, ''I am not blind to what my sister is. I ask
only that you not judge her too harshly. She has a
large curiosity and a profound romantical sense.
Hopcross is too confining for such a mind as hers.''

''It must be equally confining to yours, but I do
not see that you are selfish and uncivil in consequence.''

''Julia does not have my good fortune. If she
did, it would be otherwise with her. That is why I
cannot blame her completely and why I ask you to

see beneath her mask, as it were, and consider her unfortunate circumstances.''

''You and your sister live in the same house, the same village, the same confinement. Surely, you have not tasted much more of the life of the Town than she has. How is it possible that you have good fortune and she does not?''

Under the cover of the night, she blushed, but something about the gentleman's soft tone and the romantic surroundings prompted her to confess, ''I have my painting.''

She saw him freeze, and he seemed at a loss as to what to reply. But at least he had not teased her as his cousin had. She added with a shy laugh, ''I daresay, you recollect my drawing, such as it is, but did not know that I sometimes indulge a fancy for water-colours.''

In a measured voice, he said, ''I know nothing about such matters, but I did think you made a dashed fine daisy that day on the hill.''

Exasperated, she said, ''Why will you and your cousin persist in admiring my daisy? It was a contemptible thing, and I am sorry I ever drew it.''

''Dash it, I know nothing of such matters. If you say it is contemptible, I shall take you at your word.''

''Thank you. I wish I might persuade Mr. Bradford to do likewise. He teases me on the subject quite without mercy.''

"Well, I am dashed! James teases you on the subject? I think you misunderstand him. My cousin has never teased a lady in his life. He is the best fellow in the world, I assure you."

"He has a satirical eye, and I'm afraid he directs it at me."

"I expect he likes you very well."

"If he does, it is because he may laugh at me."

"Laugh at you?"

"Yes, on account of my paintings."

"I never heard that you had shown him your paintings."

"I did not show him my paintings, but he has seen them. At least, I feel quite sure he has. That is to say, there are occasions when I am sure of it, and others when I am sure he has not. At the moment, I am sure he has."

"This seems much ado about nothing, Miss Cassandra. Meaning no reflection upon your skill as an artist, naturally, but I am obliged to mention that my cousin has a houseful of paintings. He has seen paintings all over the world on his dashed travels. Why should he remark yours so particularly?"

"I believe he thinks they are remarkably silly."

"Are they remarkably silly?"

"There are occasions when I suspect they may be. I am afraid the world will think them so."

"The world? Ah, then you have hopes of exhibiting your pictures?"

She inhaled and said with an effort, "I confess that, yes, I should like to exhibit my paintings, but I doubt whether I shall have the opportunity—or the courage. There is nothing I dread so much as being thought ridiculous."

"Why should you be thought ridiculous?"

She lowered her eyes. "My pictures are fanciful. Some might regard them as quite wild."

After a long silence, he said, "I should like to see your paintings, if I may."

"I have never shown them to anybody."

"Well, if you do not mind showing them to an ignorant fellow who boasts little taste and less inclination to criticize, I should like to see your paintings, if I may."

She smiled at him. "That is precisely the audience which best suits me," she said.

Together they laughed. Then, suddenly conscious of the excellent understanding between them, Cassandra grew serious and said, "There is another matter we must speak of before I go."

"You are not leaving so soon?"

"I must not stay longer. But first I must address a difficult subject."

"We have dealt exceedingly well together this night. I do not think there can be anything difficult between us."

"Except the kiss you gave me in the library."

He looked at her askance. "I did not kiss you in the library."

Aghast, she cried out, "You did! You know you did!"

Suddenly, Mrs. Clapshew materialized between them. "You called me, my dear!" she said, grasping Cassandra's arms. "What has he done to you?"

"It is nothing," Cassandra assured the woman, though her agitation seemed to argue that it was not nothing.

Mrs. Clapshew turned to the gentleman. "If you attempt any rudeness of any nature whatsoever, I warn you, sir, neither your blood nor your riches will prevent me from taking my revenge. You may as well know it—I have armed myself." On that, she raised a small sack in the air.

Smiling, the gentleman enquired, "Do you mean to hit me with that, Mrs. Clapshew? It looks a vastly terrifying weapon. What is it called?"

"A sack of flour."

"What does one do with it?" he asked.

Eyeing him with scorn, she said, "One opens it up and throws it in the face of one's antagonist, blinding and confounding him; that is what one does!"

"I consider myself duly warned." Suppressing

a smile, he bowed and moved to a pillar at some
small distance.

Mrs. Clapshew turned to Cassandra. "You have
only to say the word, my dear, and I shall douse
him."

"That is very kind of you, but wholly unnecessary."

"But I heard you cry out."

"It was only that I was taken aback by something he said. It was not offensive, merely surprising."

"Oh, then I am not needed." Her disappointment was palpable.

"I am very well, I assure you."

Mrs. Clapshew started to descend the steps, then
paused a moment to enquire, "By the by, why are
you wearing a mask, my dear?"

Cassandra's hands flew to her face. "Oh, Mrs.
Clapshew. I am mortified. I can scarcely imagine
what you must think of me."

"No, no. Do not explain," said the housekeeper,
shaking her hands in the air. "I have thought better
of it. I know too much of these scandalous doings
as it is. I have no wish to know any more. I shall
merely caution you to remove the mask before you
enter the rectory. Should your parents see you, you
may frighten them out of their wits."

"You are very good, Mrs. Clapshew."

"If I were very good, I should not be here at

all. I should be in bed, my own bed, and quite alone." So saying, she faded into the night again.

Cassandra looked for the gentleman and found him lounging against a pillar, his arms folded in expectation, his lazy smile quizzing her under the bright moon. "As you were saying," he invited.

She bore down on him, thrusting her face close to his and whispering severely, "How dare you deny you kissed me. You know you did."

"I do not deny I kissed you; I merely deny it was meant as a kiss."

"That is the most unintelligible speech I have ever heard."

"Permit me to elucidate. I put my lips against your lips, that is true, and to all appearances, that constitutes a kiss. But as we agreed earlier, appearances may be deceiving. Intentions are the real heart of the matter. And my intention was not to kiss you."

"What was your intention, sir?"

"To shock your sister. To make it plain to her that I am a rogue and a villain and not to be thought of in the light of a husband. To send her into such a frenzy that she would die sooner than trust me with her heart."

"I see. You kissed me, that is to say, you pressed your lips against mine, for my sister's sake."

"Say rather for the sake of the promise I made to discourage your sister's pursuit."

"I see." Unable to explain to herself why she felt such disappointment at this explanation, she said hastily, "Well, I am vastly relieved to hear it, my lord, for, in all truthfulness, I mistook it for a kiss. Indeed, it felt to me very much like a kiss."

"Well, I'm dashed to think you mistook me so. If I had meant to kiss you, Miss Cassandra, it would have felt like this." Whereupon he leaned over and touched her lips lightly with his own, not once, but a dozen times, each time more searching and lingering than the last. She raised her hand to his cheek and was aware of his arm encircling her waist. As her lips reached for his, she heard herself sigh in contentment.

Suddenly stepping back, he put his hand to his breast, fixed a light smile to his face and said, "You see what I mean when I say that you affect me as no other woman ever has."

Cassandra could not say that she saw anything at that moment, for she was all sensation and a confusion of thoughts. The feeling that had overcome her in the library swept through her again. She had an impulse to fling her arms about his neck and abandon herself to a great many more kisses.

At the same time, a voice in her head told her that she was quite mad. The moon, or what was more likely, her own perversity, had transformed her from a sensible girl into a lunatic. Only a lunatic would put her trust in a man like Lord Marcheek, who had contrived once again to make her behave foolishly.

Summoning her wits, she said abruptly, "Good night to you, sir."

He would not permit her to leave. "Stay," he said with uncharacteristic seriousness.

Stiffly, she declared, "I will not stay. You have hoaxed me. Even while protesting your innocence, you found the means of kissing me again. I was so foolish as to be taken in by your declaration that I affect you as no other woman ever has. But I am undeceived now."

He took her hand, saying in a low voice, "I will not dishonour you or myself by denying that what I gave you just now was a kiss. I freely confess that I intended it as such. Nor can I claim to be sorry that I kissed you. It is also true that I have told many lies, but I did not lie when I said that I am a different man when I am with you. I am not the Marcheek the world knows. If you believe nothing else, believe that."

The intensity radiating through his mask was magnetic, and his words did much to mollify her. She looked at him, wishing to trust but still uncertain.

"You cannot leave while you are still angry," he said.

When she did not answer, he added, "I have no objection to standing here holding your hand the rest of the night."

"I ought to be very angry," she said quietly. "You took an oath in regard to Julia, then you played a vile trick and kissed me again. Indeed, you have done little else but play tricks the entire evening, like a cat mocking a mouse. You appeared in a mask, made hollow promises and even asked to see my paintings. I should like to believe you have been sincere, but I cannot."

"I do very much wish to see your paintings."

"You do?"

"I do."

"Please, my lord. I am not one of your Town flirts. I do not banter with ease and say things I do not mean."

"How may I convince you? Ah, I have it. I shall give you absolute proof of my sincerity."

"What proof?"

"Miss Cassandra, if you will agree to show me your paintings, I shall give you the most valuable gift that is in my power to give."

With considerable curiosity, she looked into his dark eyes. "It would be improper of me to accept a gift from you, my lord."

"This gift is not the least improper, for it is a

pledge to you that my cousin, Mr. Bradford, will henceforth and forever cease to tease you on account of your paintings. In fact, he will never mention a word on the dashed subject, unless you broach the matter yourself first.''

"How is it possible that you may guarantee your cousin's conduct?''

"If I do not make good on this promise, Miss Cassandra, then I give you permission to instruct Mrs. Clapshew to let loose the full force of her flour sack upon my head.''

She laughed. "You are mighty persuasive, my lord.''

"I shall be here at midnight tomorrow in the hope of seeing your paintings. Will you come?''

"We are not used to such late hours in the country,'' she replied, feeling shy again.

"Very well, have your rest tomorrow. Thursday, then?''

Pausing, she breathed in. Their eyes locked and remained locked for a long minute. At last, she could not resist smiling. He bowed and kissed her hand as delicately as a butterfly on a bluebell.

"Yes!'' she exclaimed, exulting. "Thursday!'' And when, with a slow, reluctant pull, she had taken her hand from his, she flew down the steps to find her chaperon.

It was with considerable perplexity that Mr. Bradford watched her go, not only because he would have liked their conversation to continue for another aeon at least, but also because Cassandra had again allowed Marcheek to kiss her. Though she had upbraided him, she had neither struck his audacious cheek nor left his side. Indeed, for one brief but unforgettable instant, she had returned Marcheek's kiss with force.

He had thought it a happy expedient to explain the discrepancy between his manner and Marcheek's by attributing it to her effect on Marcheek's hitherto invulnerable heart. To his dismay, she had accepted this explanation. She believed that he was Marcheek, and not just Marcheek, but ironically, the *real* Marcheek, the good man beneath the scoundrel's mask. What, then, had his clever deception accomplished? Merely this: that he had persuaded her that underneath Marcheek's exterior lay a feeling and intelligent man with strong, though well-hidden, principles of honour and gentleness. The next time she saw Marcheek, she would seek his eyes, draw him into conversation and throw him glances of adoration. She would not be able to withstand his charms. She would be head over ears in love with him, if she wasn't already. Marcheek would have nobody but his cousin James to thank for this good fortune, while his cousin James would have nobody but himself to blame.

Chapter Nine

Regarding Matrimony

Mrs. Vickery scarcely recognized her second daughter the next day. Whereas Cassandra customarily rose betimes and, before breakfasting, visited the bakehouse, inspected the larder, gathered the eggs from the henhouse, practised the pianoforte and worked at a painting, on Wednesday morning she slept well past midday. Worried, her mother woke her by putting a cool hand to her forehead and asking, "Are you unwell today, my poor dear?"

Slowly Cassandra opened her eyes and treated her mother to a dazzling smile. "I have never been better, Mama."

"There is no need to keep the truth from me," Mrs. Vickery said. "If you are ill, you must tell me so that I may send for Dr. Suckling. You certainly look more owlish than usual today."

Cassandra answered with an extravagant stretch of the arms. "Please do not put Dr. Suckling to the trouble for nothing. I am not only well, I am perfect." To prove the truth of this assertion, she jumped out of her bed and began to dance to the accompaniment of "Sir Roger de Coverley," which she trilled at the top of her lungs. This behaviour did nothing to soothe her mother's fears for her health.

"You are excessively odd today," Mrs. Vickery observed.

For some reason known only to herself, this remark delighted Cassandra. She smiled broadly, hugged her mother with fervour and declared, "I am as hungry as a plough horse."

"Illness is no excuse for vulgarity, dear. I shall send up a cup of coffee and a biscuit for you."

"Oh, Mama, just today I wish I might breakfast on bacon, bread and jam, fritters and chocolate."

Alarmed, Mrs. Vickery took Cassandra by the shoulders. "What ails you, child? It is Julia who behaves in such a manner. You have always been as steady as Gibraltar. Tell me what the matter is, or I shall send you back to your bed straightaway."

Blinking, Cassandra answered, "Nothing is the matter. I know only that it is the loveliest day I have ever beheld."

"It is raining."

Prancing to the window, Cassandra pulled aside

the curtain and sighed contentedly. "Yes, it is raining. How prodigiously, how vastly, how amazingly
beautiful the rain is."

"And how wet. The roads will be full of pot-
holes and mud. There will be no walking to the
village today."

This information failed to depress Cassandra's
spirits. Her mother, in exasperation, was required
to leave the girl without discovering the source of
her unaccountable behaviour.

Vaguely aware that she was alone, Cassandra
sang as she donned her stockings and shift, exulting in the certainty that there could not possibly
exist a creature as blessed as herself. Although she
could not be said to be flying about, rescuing foundering ships and their handsome captains, she felt
she was living the adventures she painted. The
same exhilaration she ordinarily felt on Marietta's
behalf, she now felt on her own. It was more than
she had ever dared to dream would happen.

The fears she had experiencd whenever she recollected Lord Marcheek's reputation were now dis-
pelled. She was working a change in him, he had
said; when he was with her, he was a different
man. She believed that he was speaking the truth,
that his words were not merely for the sake of seduction, for when he was alone with her, he was
not the fribble she had observed him to be in company. When he was with her, he was able to reveal

himself as a man who could wax poetic at the sight of the stars, speak in earnest and regard her through his mask with genuine and undisguised feeling. Of course, she had to confess that what he had said had flattered her vanity; nothing appealed to her so much as the notion of bringing out the noble sentiments in an acknowledged rogue. Vanity aside, however, she was moved beyond measure by his unexpected marks of consideration. His asking Mrs. Clapshew to be her chaperon, for example, had been more than gallant; it had been sweet. She cherished that sweetness. He had not been so gallant or so sweet to Julia when he had agreed to meet her in the library at Cantywell.

Julia! She sank onto the bed at the thought of her sister, who hitherto had not entered her mind for a single second. The heat of shame flushed her face as she realized that the night before she had entirely forgotten Julia, even though her purpose had supposedly been to protect her. Far from protecting her, she had allowed herself to be kissed by the man her sister wanted. She was overcome with remorse and chagrin at this realization, especially because she had always held it as an article of faith that it was one's duty to keep one's promises, just as she had always believed it was wrong to encourage a gentleman that one's sister was setting her cap for. Worst of all was the fact that in spite of her remorse, she did not wish to give Marcheek up.

Her earlier joy now turned to wormwood as she contemplated the enormities she had committed. If Julia had been near, Cassandra would have run to her, confessed her perfidy and thrown herself on her mercy. With Julia at Sparrowdene, though, she scarely knew what to do. Would it be cowardly to send her a confession in a letter? Ought she to wait until Julia returned so that she might tell her in person? How would she face her sister when next they met?

She threw herself on the bed, put her head under the pillow and burrowed her wet cheeks into the flannel, as if the answer to her dilemma lay buried in the patchwork quilt she and Julia had made together.

When she left her daughter, Mrs. Vickery descended the stairs, shaking her head in bewilderment. Then an idea struck her, an idea inspired by the arrival of Ned Bumpers, who announced to her in a spasm of head flutters that he had splendid news for Miss Cassandra.

"I do not know that she is quite well," the mother said, welcoming her daughter's beau. "She has such a fine, delicate constitution. Girls of her good nature and industriousness sometimes suffer fatigue and headache."

Ned's alarm at this news pleased Mrs. Vickery. His head wagged twice as fast as usual and his eyes bulged. ''Have you sent for Dr. Suckling?'' he cried.

''Cassandra will not permit even her own mother to fuss, I fear, and so she refuses to have Dr. Suckling. Such a brave girl, the disposition of an angel. She will make an excellent wife.''

''Perhaps I ought to come back another day, when she is disposed to receive callers.''

''No, Mr. Bumpers. You must stay.'' She bustled him to a chair in the parlour and induced him to sit, saying all the while, ''Your visit will enliven her. Poor girl. She is in need of company to raise her spirits. Ill health makes one so dreadfully low. I shall have Susan go and fetch her.''

Before he could protest, she sent the housemaid abovestairs with instructions to bring Cassandra to her at once. She then seated herself near the young man so that if he had any notion of making his escape, she would be on the spot to prevent it.

With a slow step and a woeful expression, Cassandra entered the parlour. The dejection with which she greeted Ned confirmed Mrs. Vickery's suspicion that her daughter was in love. The child bore all the signs of it: sleeping well into the morning, humming, dancing, rhapsodizing over the rain, then plunging into the depths of despair. The mother had seen the very same symptoms in her eldest daughter a hundred times. Therefore, after sitting a moment with the young people and thanking the gentleman for the honour he had conferred on her poor house by his visit, she deftly excused herself and left them to themselves.

"I am desolate to hear you are ill," Ned began.

"Ill? Wherever did you hear such a hum?"

"Your mother was kind enough to tell me and to say that I might stay and visit."

"Please do not pity me, Mr. Bumpers. I am frightfully well, never better."

"I am not surprised to hear you say so. Your mother confided to me that you are amazingly good-natured and uncomplaining, though you are frequently plagued with headaches and fatigue. I do admire your courage, Miss Cassandra, being so entirely lacking in that quality myself."

Cassandra sighed and resigned herself to being thought a martyr.

His head bobbing rhythmically, Ned went on, "I would not have disturbed your convalescence if I'd known how it was with you, but I came with news, Miss Cassandra, news which I hope will please you."

"If it is pleasing to you, Mr. Bumpers, it will please me."

"Oh, that is what I had hoped you would say, for the news is very pleasing to me, and it is this: I have persuaded my parents that it would be unwise for us to visit Bath in September, or, indeed, at any time.''

Genuinely sorry to hear that her neighbours were not to have the pleasure of travelling to a place of which they had all heard so much, she did not smile but instead said, ''That is too bad. I made sure you would have a most delightful Season in Bath.''

''Dear me, I thought you would be pleased.''

''Well, if you did not wish to go to Bath, then I suppose I am pleased for you.''

''But you do not sound pleased. I thought you would be, that like your sister, you regarded Bath as unfashionable and not nearly so amusing as London.''

''It does not matter what pleases me, or what pleases Julia. What pleases you, Mr. Bumpers?''

Here he looked confused. ''What pleases me?''

''Surely you have a preference for one place over another. Surely you have thought to yourself from time to time that you might like to visit the seaside or a spa or Town or the Lake Country or some other spot which has sparked your fancy and inspired daydreams of adventure.''

''No, never.''

Cassandra could not believe that any human creature could fail to imagine some sort of adventure, however pale. ''Do you mean to say that you have never longed to visit a place that you have never seen before, some place far distant, where the manners and the people are entirely different from what you are accustomed to?''

"Well, I do like to visit you and your family when I may. And I have even been to Sparrowdene to pay my respects to Miss Vickery. It was she who suggested that I might do better not to go to Bath at all.''

Earnestly, Cassandra said, "You must not rely upon what others say. You must listen to your own heart and obey its promptings. That is what I intend to do.''

He swallowed hard, thrust his chin at her, and looked doubtful.

"I know I am right, Mr. Bumpers. There is in you, there is in every human creature, a natural tendency to wish, to dream, to imagine, to long. If your dream is some great adventure, no matter how ridiculous or unseemly it may appear in the eyes of the world, you must pursue it.''

"I must?''

"If you do not, you will never forgive yourself.''

He shuddered.

"Whether it be a season in Bath or some other yearning that has long lain hidden in your bosom, you must not let it wither and die. You must seize your opportunity, no matter the consequences.''

"Oh, my love, my divine one!'' he blurted out

ardently. Seizing her hand, he fell to his knees on the carpet and implored, "If you will be my wife, then you may decide where it is best to spend the Season. Bath, London, it is all one to me. You would please me most by pleasing yourself. I detest having to choose where it is I wish to go, for I never know, but I should be the happiest creature on Earth to have you tell me. Will you, therefore, accept my hand and heart in marriage?"

Snatching her hand away, Cassandra said, "Mr. Bumpers, get up at once. You have taken leave of your senses."

"Yes, but only because you told me to. You said I must seize my opportunity. I hope you are not angry with me. I cannot abide it when anybody is angry with me, especially you. I should never have presumed to propose marriage if you had not insisted that I seize my opportunity, no matter the consequences."

"I was speaking of travel!"

He performed a chicken flutter and replied, "I had hoped you were speaking of love."

On that, Cassandra blushed mightily, for it appeared to her now that she had indeed been speaking of love. She put her hand to her mouth as the realization struck her that she had been thinking of Lord Marcheek when she had spoken. She had fallen in love with him and, though it was patently obvious, had been blind to the fact until this moment. Then, recovering her equanimity, she noticed that Ned still waited on his knees. He bobbed his head patiently until she should vouchsafe him a reply.

"Oh, Ned, please do get up," she said earnestly. "You will give your leg a spasm."

"You called me Ned." He grinned bashfully.

"I addressed you as Ned because when a gentleman proposes marriage to a lady, she knows that he esteems her as a friend."

The up-turned corners of his smile now fell. "I did not wish to esteem you as a friend. I wished to have you as my bride. I had hoped that was why you called me Ned, because you saw no harm in the scheme."

"I called you Ned because, though I am obliged to refuse your amiable offer, I am very flattered by it."

"Could you not call me Mr. Bumpers and accept my offer?"

"I am afraid I could not."

He sighed. "Your sister assured me that if I did not go to so unfashionable a place as Bath, any girl of sense would consider an offer of marriage from me."

"I wish you would tell Julia to speak for herself alone. I have no quarrel with Bath."

"Would you prefer to go to London?"

Throwing up her hands she cried, "I cannot decide where it is you are to go. If you are looking for an authority on that subject, you must apply to Julia again. I incite a legion of woes whenever I poke my nose into concerns that are none of my affair. Wherever you go, I shall wish you a safe and happy journey, but I shall be unable to accompany you as your wife.''

With an effort, he rose and brushed off his pantaloons. ''You are not angry with me?'' he enquired.

''No, I am not angry.''

''Will you be angry if I return at some future date to renew my offer?''

''Not angry, but piqued perhaps.''

He considered the risk and concluded, ''As it is my greatest wish to please you in all things, I shall do exactly as you say, but as you have said a great many things today, I daresay I shall forget a vast deal of them.'' With that, he performed a creditable bow and bobbed on his way.

Unlike Cassandra, Mr. Bradford awoke neither late nor cheerful. The events of the previous evening served to trouble his sleep and set him to pacing the hall, his boots echoing on the flagstones, his face taut, his thoughts engrossed. Thus he was discovered by Lord Marcheek, who entered at the great door, swaying a little owing to the effects of an excessively merry night at The Star and Garter, and hanging on to the neck of the footman who opened the door to him.

"James," his lordship called out, causing the footman to wince at the aroma of his breath. "Dashed kind of you to wait up for me, but wholly unnecessary, for I am going to bed this instant and I shall sleep a fortnight." He placed his head on the footman's shoulder and commenced to snore.

Mr. Bradford smiled ruefully at the wreck who stood, or rather slumped, before him. He rescued the footman by draping his cousin's arm over his own shoulder and hauling him towards the stairs.

Finding himself moving, Marcheek awoke.

"I trust you had a splendid evening," Mr. Bradford greeted him. "How much did you lose?"

As he permitted himself to be coaxed up the stairs, his lordship replied in an offended tone, "Why do you always assume that I have lost? It is impossible for a man to lose all the time. Can you lend me fifty, James?"

Having attained the landing, Mr. Bradford steered in the direction of Marcheek's bedchamber. "I smell something foul," he remarked, "and I suspect it is you."

Marcheek laughed. "I suspect you are right. I spent a dashed pleasant hour in the stable with a dashed pleasant companion. But you needn't alarm yourself about her, James. She is not a respectable young lady, so no harm will come of it. Hope your evening was also, shall we say, satisfactory?''

After depositing his cousin on the bed, Mr. Bradford pulled off his boots. "It was the very devil," he replied.

Marcheek permitted himself to be divested of his coat and the straw that clung to his hair. "You ought to have come with me, James. It was a great mistake to meet this lady, whoever she is. As you have warned me time and again, nothing good can come of such meetings."

"I ought to have heeded my own advice, for, deuce take me, I am in love with her."

Astounded, Marcheek sat up. The movement dizzied him, however, and he was obliged to fall back onto the pillows. "Poor James. With your dashed confounded ideas, I expect you will next think of marrying the creature."

"I should like nothing better than to marry her, only she will not have me."

"Dash it, James, you are too gloomy. You are a catch, coz. Any lady would be glad to get her clutches into you. After all, you are the heir to a baronetcy, as rich as old Midas himself, well travelled, a gentleman of conversation when you are not being tedious or lecturing and you are not ill-looking, either, thanks to your resemblance to me.''

"Oblige me, Marcheek, and do not attempt to be heartening."

"I cannot believe the lady does not love you."

"She loves another man."

"Well, if she is too much of a dunce to know she ought to love you, then you had better put her from your mind altogether and come with me to The Star and Garter, just as soon as I have recovered from this last visit. Oh, my poor head. It will not cease sounding a tattoo in my ears."

"Do not tell me to put her from my mind because I cannot. Devil knows I've tried. And I will thank you not to call her a dunce. If she is not in love with me, it is because she is in love with you, heaven help her."

Marcheek grinned loosely as he lolled on the bed. "The ladies are all mad for me, it's true. I do not know how I have come to deserve such fortune, but that, alas, is my lot." He nestled under the coverlet and declared with a sigh, "I must bear my fate as bravely as I can."

"The reason she is in love with you, cousin," Mr. Bradford said, loosening Marcheek's cravat, "is that she thinks that *I* am you. I dressed and spoke so as to make her think it and, to my infinite regret, I succeeded."

His lordship's eyelids lowered as he grew drowsy. "In that case, James, I should like to borrow five hundred. If you are going to use my clothes and my name, I demand to be compensated. I shall not be greedy, especially as you are a near relation. A mere six or seven hundred will do, guineas not pounds, you understand.''

"You must go to sleep now," Mr. Bradford said, closing his cousin's mouth, which had fallen open, "and I must go to Pilkingdown Rectory. If there is a way out of this lie, I have got to find it.''

Three small heads appeared behind the stone fence surrounding the rectory. Mr. Bradford saw two of the Vickery boys and their little sister scale the fence and jump down to intercept him on his approach.

"Oh, there is such a row!" declared the girl, who slipped her hand into Mr. Bradford's to lead him to the gate.

The boys, resenting her proprietary manner with their favourite, hovered close to his other side, and to improve upon their sister's information, reported, "Cassie is to be banished to her room until she is restored to her senses. That is what Mama says.''

Mr. Bradford stopped. "Miss Cassandra is in some difficulty?''

The three exchanged glances and titters. "Mama quarrels with her because she will not have Mr. Bumpers.'' On that, the three of them walked about in the manner of chickens, squawking and clucking in chorus.

"Mr. Bumpers proposed marriage to your sister, I collect. But are you certain she will not accept him?

"She will be compelled to accept him, Mama says. Papa will make her have him. Mama says if he does not, he will never know another moment's peace in his own house."

"I see," he said darkly. Quickening his pace, he bade the children goodbye and entered the gate. After several insistent knocks, he was admitted to the house by the distracted housemaid, who led him to the parlour and announced him in the middle of what was clearly a bitter quarrel between Mr. and Mrs. Vickery and their second daughter.

The three stared transfixed at the visitor. Their open mouths informed him that he had interrupted their shouting.

Mr. Bradford handed his hat to the housemaid and smiled at them all. "Good day to you," he said amiably. "I trust I find you all well."

Mrs. Vickery was the first to remember what civility required of her. He was induced to sit and did so with every appearance of ignorance as to the circumstances upon which he had intruded.

Cassandra sank onto the chair near the little writing table and gazed out the window, while her father, claiming business at the church, went away grumbling, but not before warning Cassandra that he would have more to say to her hereafter.

"How kind of you to honour our poor parlour with an unexpected visit," Mrs. Vickery said with false cheer.

"It is I who am honoured," Mr. Bradford replied, glancing at Cassandra, who did not appear to hear.

"You will excuse Mr. Vickery's hurrying away. He is quite worn out with care. He suffers from palpitations. I fear I shall soon suffer an attack of the megrims myself." Her eyes fell on Cassandra, who, her expression seemed to say, was the cause of this sudden epidemic in her family.

"Mrs. Vickery," said Mr. Bradford soothingly, "permit me to entreat you to have a care for yourself. Your prodigious hospitality induces you to stay to entertain me, I know, but I should feel obliged to you if you regarded me as a friend and well-wisher, which is what I am, and looked to your headache instead of to me. If you wish to retire, do not stay on my account."

Tempted by this invitation, the lady said, "But there is only Cassandra here to entertain you."

"I shall just have a word with her and then take my leave."

Sighing, Mrs. Vickery rose from her chair and said, "You are too good, Mr. Bradford. I hope

Cassandra will do everything that is proper to see to your welcome.''

The object of this hope neither moved nor gave any indication that she was listening.

Shaking her head in despair, Mrs. Vickery went out of the room calling for Susan and a vinaigrette.

Before he spoke, Mr. Bradford contemplated Cassandra's profile. Its lines had never failed to charm him in the past. Now he admired the stubbornness of her chin and the intelligence of her brow. He had every confidence that she would hold firm against the blandishments of her parents, but given that the last thing he wished was to see her married to somebody else, he determined to do whatever was in his power to shore up her resolve. To that end, he said gently, ''The children tell me you have refused Mr. Bumpers.''

She turned to him with a look of mortification. ''They ought not to have troubled you with our family concerns.''

''I am glad they did.''

''If you mean to offer sympathy, I wish you would think better of it, sir. It would be best not to speak of it at all.''

''I do not mean to offend you with an offer of sympathy. I mean to offer assistance.''

She shook her head. ''I am sure your intention is to be kind, but with your permission, we will speak of something else. What think you of books?

Have you read *Clarentine?* The conduct of the heroine is most unnatural, in my view. Her difficulties are entirely forced. I have read the tale six times through and have yet to find any merit in it.''

He moved close to the table and when she looked up at him, he said, ''I know nothing of *Clarentine,* but I do know that I should be honoured to assist you, if you will allow me to.''

After a pause, during which her emotion was evident, she replied, ''I do not think there is any conceivable assistance that you or anybody can render.''

''There is,'' he said. ''It is the simplest thing in the world.''

This caused her to raise her brows and regard him with complete bafflement.

''All you need do,'' he said smoothly, ''is to inform your parents that I, too, have proposed marriage to you.''

Chapter Ten

Declarations

Cassandra remained perfectly still, regarding Mr. Bradford in bewilderment. To be certain she had heard him aright, she asked, "You advise me to say to my parents that you have proposed marriage to me?"

"Yes."

She rose, eased past him and put some distance between them by walking to the mantel, where she studied a painted plate. His pleasant smile, ease of manner and the preposterous nature of the suggestion persuaded her that he was not serious. "You are quizzing me, I collect," she replied.

"Not at all. I expect your mother and father will cease to press you to accept Mr. Bumpers once they hear that you have better prospects."

She was compelled to acknowledge that her parents would regard Mr. Bradford as a more desirable catch than Ned Bumpers, for the former represented a future title and fortune, whereas the latter was a mere "Mister" with a handsome competence. But she could not help suspecting that Mr. Bradford's purpose in proposing such an outlandish strategem was not exclusively to save her from being pressed to marry Ned Bumpers. He meant also to tease, she was convinced. After all, he had never shown any partiality towards her up to now. The attentions he had paid her had been prompted, as far as she could tell, merely by politeness, boredom or a desire to tweak. Even now, as she stole a glimpse at his face, he appeared to regard her without any sentiment stronger than amiability.

"You will think me very dull, sir," she said at last, "but I do not follow your logic. My telling Mama and Papa that I am considering your proposal will certainly purchase me a modicum of peace, but only for a brief period. Eventually they will wish to know when you and I are to be married. What am I to tell them then?"

"Set any date you fancy. I shall not object."

"I see. And what happens when the fateful day arrives?"

"Why, we marry, naturally."

Stunned, she steadied herself on the post of the mantel. "Mr. Bradford, are you proposing a strategem to ward off my parents' coercion, or are you proposing marriage to me?''

''Both.''

She closed her eyes, than opened them again. ''This is folly. A man does not marry in order to rescue a woman from the governance of her mother and father. This is more of your Town wit, I collect.''

Hotly, he came to her and said, ''I should think a young lady of your good sense might be able to distinguish between a jest and a proposal of marriage.''

With a gesture of helplessness, she said, ''I never in my life imagined you truly had marriage in view.''

''Why should I not have marriage in view?'' he retorted. ''I love you. I admire you. I have done since I first set eyes on you, and I wish to continue to set eyes on you for the rest of my life.''

Her cheeks flushed as she realized that Mr. Bradford was entirely serious. For once, it was clear that he was neither quizzing nor laughing at her. She was stunned to think that he loved her, had loved her all this time, and she was humbled by the realization that she had misunderstood him, that the words and conduct she had attributed to satire had in fact been prompted by love.

With soft compassion she said, ''I am greatly honoured by your regard, Mr. Bradford, and if circumstances permitted, I should certainly do my best to learn to hold you in that esteem which every husband desires and deserves. But I cannot love you.''

The stark look he gave her made her avoid his gaze. As she turned away, tears blurred her vision. She not only felt sorry to have wounded him, but she suddenly felt the enormity of what she was doing—refusing not one but two suitors in the space of an afternoon, and not two ordinary suitors but two who loved her and wished to place their fates and their fortunes at her feet.

Even Marietta, the most beautiful and daring sea nymph ever to launch an adventure, had not received two such proposals in a single day.

''I am aware you do not love me now,'' Mr. Bradford said in a measured voice, ''but I have every confidence that when you know me better, you will return my regard.''

He spoke with such an effort that her heart went out to him. Summoning her strength, she faced him. There was a depth of intensity in his expression that melted her. His handsomeness was not marred in the least by his gravity.

Indeed, she felt that if she were not already in love, she might in time come to love Mr. Bradford. Sighing for the pain she must inflict, however unintentionally, she resolved to confide to him something of the truth. Accordingly, she said, ''I esteem you too highly to deceive you. It is true I might come to love you, Mr. Bradford, but for one obstacle—my heart is already engaged. I have placed my affections with a gentleman who makes it impossible for me to entertain the thought of marrying anybody else.'' She bowed her head, then raised it to see what effect her words had on him. Oddly enough, he did not appear unduly perturbed.

''May I ask the fortunate gentleman's name?''

She blushed. ''You may not.''

''You are engaged to him?''

''No.''

''He has spoken of marriage, however?''

Again, a flush of heat filled her cheeks. ''He has not.''

''But you believe he will ask you to be his wife?''

''I do not know.''

''If I may venture to say so, this does not bode well, Miss Cassandra.''

''You are right, of course, but I cannot help it.''

''But suppose this gentleman has lied to you. Suppose he has merely pretended to be serious. Suppose he is indulging in a flirtation while you imagine he intends marriage. Suppose he only means to deceive you.''

His words resurrected the fears she had permitted to be put to rest. Cassandra swallowed with difficulty and took a sharp breath. ''In such an instance,'' she said, ''I do not know what would become of me. I detest a liar and could not soon forgive him—or myself for believing him.''

It moved her to see his pained expression.

He took her hand, raised it to his breast and, opening her palm, kissed it. ''If this nameless gentleman should break your heart,'' he said with a passion she had never witnessed in him, ''he shall have to answer to me.''

Thursday passed at a snail's pace. At last, after the children had been sent to the nursery, the rest of the family, consisting of Mr. and Mrs. Vickery and Cassandra, supped on a tray in the parlour. The parents cast gloomy looks in Cassandra's direction and punctuated their silence with encomiums on Ned Bumpers and warnings that she might live out her life as a spinster—lonely, laughed at and dependent on an allowance from one of her brothers. Had their remarks been of longer duration, she might have revealed that she had received another proposal. As it was, she merely had to endure their scowls for an hour, after which she retired in disgrace to her chamber.

For consolation, she went to the chest in which she kept her paintings and scrutinized each in turn. There were eleven in all, a far cry from the fifty that had been destroyed. Though they were few in number, she felt that they were finer than her earlier work. One of them pictured Marietta seated regally on the back of a dragonfly. In her hands, she held the reins that directed her mount on his flight across a pink sky towards a wondrous city. Another showed the sea nymph nestled in the petals of a rose, asleep. A third portrayed her kneeling on the shores of a pond, admiring her reflection. On her head she wore a hat fashioned from an obliging honey bee.

Though she kept at her occupation for some time, Cassandra's emotions would not be soothed. Mr. Bradford's words came back to her, and she began to doubt the wisdom of showing her work to Lord Marcheek. Why had she felt the impulse to take him into her confidence, she wondered. Suppose he had lied to her, as Mr. Bradford suggested? Suppose he intended nothing but flirtation? She trembled to think how readily she had permitted her heart to trust him, how readily she had betrayed her sister for his sake. Perhaps her only reason for trusting him was that she wished to. Perhaps she had been captivated by the romance of their meetings, especially by the masks, which permitted her to be more herself than when she appeared before the world fully revealed, and which, by preventing her from reading his expressions with her intellect, had enabled her to sense his meanings with her heart. Such sensations could be dangerously seductive.

Resolutely, she dismissed her doubts. She knew why she trusted him: because her instinct told her that he truly loved her. A man's reputation was not necessarily founded in truth. After all, she herself was reputed to be quiet and prim, and was not that the very opposite of what she was? Unless he gave her actual cause to do otherwise, she could continue to trust him, despite her own misgivings and Mr. Bradford's insinuations.

The household was as quiet as a graveyard when she crept from the rectory. She wore a shawl over her hair and the mask of peacock-blue feathers. Under her arm, she carried her packet of paintings tied up in a ribbon. Although she was conscious that she appeared very odd and would be thought quite mad if she were to be seen, she did not turn back.

As before, Mrs. Clapshew met her. Instead of leading her to the temple, however, she escorted Cassandra into Kirkingdell Lane. They followed this path for some minutes, sheltered from view by the shadow cast by hawthorne hedges. The chestnuts and yews in the distance were black against the night, which was lent an eerie grey aura by the moonlight that played on the clouds.

''Where are we going?'' Cassandra enquired.

''Have no fear,'' the housekeeper assured her. ''I have brought my sack of flour.''

They left the lane and proceeded in the direction

of a stand of poplars. Cassandra was aware of the perfume the previous day's rain had produced in the air, of the rustle of branches close to her ear, the crackle of twigs under her boots and the warmth of the summer night. Inhaling deeply, she wondered how she might translate such ravishing splendour into a painting.

At last they paused at the gatehouse, which stood outside the Gothic stone entrance to Cantywell. In former times, the house had boasted a liveried gatekeeper who had greeted visitors and directed them along the approach to the house, but as the present marquess had adopted many of the unceremonious customs of his simple neighbours, he had dispensed with that office two decades earlier.

The gatehouse was constructed of sturdy red brick and a slate roof. Before Mrs. Clapshew had the opportunity to knock at its weatherworn door, it opened and a gentleman filled the entry way. He wore the sombrero and flowing cloak that gave him, in Cassandra's eyes, a dashing and dangerous air, an air that was enhanced by the fact that once again he was masked.

With a gesture of welcome, he invited the ladies inside. Cassandra thought the single room bore the signs of recent hasty dusting and washing. On the table, a lantern dimly burned. Rough wooden chairs had been arranged about the table to make the room resemble a parlour.

Mrs. Clapshew settled herself into a chair that creaked under her amplitude. She drew her cloak around her and crossed her arms, fixing her eyes on the gentleman as though ready to spring in an instant, if need be.

"Please make yourself easy," the gentleman invited the housekeeper. "I take my oath, I shall conduct myself like a saint."

To which she replied, "You are not so high and mighty that I would not give you a dousing if you required it."

Laughing, he said, "If you persist in threatening me, Mrs. Clapshew, it is certain to give rise to talk in the neighbourhood. The gossips will say you are in love with me. Nothing looks so much like violent affection as violent hatred."

The lady harrumphed and sniffed and hugged the flour sack to her bosom.

The gentleman took Cassandra's hand to lead her to a chair, then drew another close to hers. "No doubt you wish to know why I have brought you to this ancient gatehouse in the middle of the night," he said.

"Yes."

"If I am to see your paintings, I must be able to rely on more than moonlight." He turned up the light in the lantern.

Looking about her, Cassandra noted that the windows had been well covered.

"I see you have brought them," he said.

"Yes." She set her packet of pasteboards on the table. As he untied the ribbon, she glanced anxiously at Mrs. Clapshew.

"Have no fear," he said. "Mrs. Clapshew has sworn not to peek."

Hearing herself spoken of, the lady raised her eyes heavenward and vowed, "I am not one to poke my nose where it does not belong, or misbehave, unlike some folk I might mention, who parted company with sense and prudence long ago."

Cassandra met the gentleman's eyes, and they smiled at this powerful disapproval. True to her word, Mrs. Clapshew made no move to peek; however, she did keep a sharp eye out for the progress of the courtship she so much wished to promote.

When he had sorted through the paintings, occasionally holding one close to the light of the lantern, Cassandra could not resist asking, "What is your opinion?"

At first, he seemed lost in thought. Then, collecting himself, he replied, "Dash it all, I know nothing of such matters and, therefore, can have no opinion."

"Well, at least you have not laughed at them."

"Laughed? No, I do not find them laughable."

Then, as an afterthought, he added, "In fact, I should say they are dashed pretty in their way."

"You do not find them wild and fantastical?"

"I do not know. The light is exceedingly poor. Perhaps I ought to take them to Cantywell tonight so that I may look at them in the daylight tomorrow."

She grew distressed. "I have never let them out of my possession."

"Do not be alarmed. I shall take excellent care of them."

"But suppose somebody should come upon them."

"By 'somebody', you no doubt refer to James. I can promise you that I shall keep them as safe as though they were under lock and key. My cousin will never set eyes on them."

She shook her head and looked doubtful.

He smiled. "Miss Cassandra," he enquired, "did my dashed cousin call on you today?"

Startled by the change of subject, she said, "Why, yes."

"And did he tweak you on the subject of your art?"

"He did not allude to it at all."

"So you see, I am a gentleman of my word. I promised he would keep mum and that is what he has done. And if I promise that my dashed cousin shall not set eyes on your paintings, you may be certain he shan't."

Still she hesitated.

"By the by," he said, "as James was silent on the subject of your pictures, what did he have to say for himself?"

Her blush was so hot that she knew he must have seen it. "He proposed marriage to me," she confessed.

Rising, he laughed. "Whatever possessed him to do such an outlandish thing, I wonder?"

She stood, as well, a little abashed at his laughter. "He loves me," she replied.

"You mean he *says* he loves you. There is often a difference, as I am sure you are aware, between what a gentleman says and what he feels. It is a difference which I observe frequently in my own conduct."

Uneasily, she answered, "I am well aware of the difference, but I believe Mr. Bradford meant what he said."

At this, Mrs. Clapshew emitted a grunt, which the others ignored.

"You believed him? And why is that? I had thought you suspected him of laughing at you."

"I do not know why I believed him. Perhaps it was his air. It lacked any hint of teasing and laughing. He was as solemn as I have ever seen him."

The gentleman approached until his eyes were

no more than an inch from hers. His white mask and soft smiling lips were spellbinding. In a silky voice, he said, "It is no wonder he was solemn. Even a dashed scoundrel like myself would forget to breathe, let alone laugh and tease, in your company. The glow of your eyes must rob any man of shallow airs."

He spoke so earnestly that she drew closer. Raising her hand, he kissed her fingertips.

Cassandra found she could not swallow. The most she could do was to return his steadfast gaze.

Suddenly he laughed and let drop her hand. "You see how easy it is to appear sincere, Miss Cassandra. Even I can do it. In point of fact, I practise my sincerity a good deal, like my dance steps. There is nothing the ladies like better than believing a gentleman is sincere."

She recoiled. "You were joking just now?"

"What a pity it is so difficult to know when a man is merely joking."

She moved away, puzzled. There was a cruelty in his tone which hurt her. Until that moment, she had not thought Lord Marcheek capable of deliberate unkindness.

He rubbed his hands as though in satisfaction. "My felicitations to you, Miss Cassandra. You have snared a prize catch, indeed. My cousin James has never before proposed marriage to anybody—that I am aware of. Pray tell me, what arts did you employ to persuade him to overcome his reticence?''

Incensed, she retorted, ''I did not employ arts. I do not have the least idea why Mr. Bradford proposed, or why he should love me. Indeed, I find it incredible that he does, for he is a man of the world and quite handsome and even amusing when he chooses to be. He might have any number of ladies for his wife, I am certain. His choosing me is the most perplexing thing.''

He remarked with a smile and a shrug, ''If he loves you, as he claims, I wonder why he wishes to go and spoil it by marrying you?''

There was an edge to his voice that chilled her. ''You are cynical in matters of love,'' she said.

''Not in the least. I am able to love as devotedly as the next fellow. Love is the most amusing thing I know, with the possible exception of *vingt-et-un* and *chemin de fer*. It is marriage I object to. I myself do not intend to marry for forty years at the very least.''

''Oh,'' she said, with a sinking heart.

''And when are the nuptials to take place?''

''Nuptials?''

''Yes, the marriage between Miss Cassandra Vickery and my esteemed cousin.''

''I refused him,'' she said unhappily.

''What? Refused James Bradford, who is destined soon to become a fourth baronet, the master of Dimmesdale and its vast estates, the richest fellow in Warwickshire and a dashed handsome and charming one to boot? You refused this paragon?''

Bowing her head, she confessed she had.

''What caused you to do such a foolish thing?''

''I do not love him,'' she said simply.

''I had thought a young lady always felt *obliged* to love a gentleman who was wealthy, eligible and, above all, willing.''

Her temper flared. ''Not if she is already in love with somebody else!''

He grasped her shoulders and said with intensity, ''You ought not to love anybody else. You ought to love James.''

Near to tears, she cried, ''I should like nothing better than to love him. Unfortunately, I love his cousin.''

Roughly, he let her go. ''Damn!'' He walked towards the window.

She snapped, ''I did not intend it as an insult.''

''You ought not to love his cousin.''

Mrs. Clapshew interjected here, ''Listen well, Miss Cassandra. He speaks God's own truth, pure and simple.''

Ignoring the housekeeper, Cassandra marched to the gentleman and said passionately, ''I shall teach myself not to love you, if you like. But I will not accept Mr. Bradford. He deserves to have a wife who can love him with a whole heart. As to you, my lord, I hope you may find every happiness with the true object of your affection: a pack of cards.'' Then she ran to the door, pulled it open and fled into the night.

Although tears nearly blinded her, she quickly retraced her steps towards the lane. Her face was flushed with anger; her breast rose and fell as she breathed. Mr. Bradford had been right. The man she had permitted herself to love had been merely playing with her, flirting, amusing himself with her whenever he could not devote himself to gaming. It occurred to her that if Julia had witnessed the proceedings of the past minutes, she would have taken great satisfaction in knowing that the first wish of her heart, to be revenged on her sister, had been granted. Cassandra had been amply repaid for her perfidy by words cruel and cold enough to sting her for years to come.

So rapt was she in painful reflections that she was taken wholly by surprise when her arm was seized. Abruptly, she was forced to halt. Turning, she saw the mask of white satin and behind it, eyes that burned.

''What do you want with me?'' she implored. ''You have already said every brutal thing you could say. What more do you wish?''

''You have forgotten your dashed pictures,'' he said. ''You must come back for them.''

She froze. After years of keeping her paintings

secret and protected, she had suddenly forgotten them entirely. Mortified, she scarcely knew what to say. She did not wish to return to the gatehouse to collect them, but she certainly did not wish to leave them in the hands of a man who appeared to be every inch the rogue and villain she had first thought him. "You need not have come after me," she said at last. "You may have them sent to the rectory."

"That will not do. You will be uneasy the rest of your days, wondering who might have peeked at them. No, you had better return to the gatehouse and gather them together yourself."

With a gesture of helpless confusion, she cried, "You are a complete puzzle. One moment you act the scoundrel's part and the next you wish to protect my paintings from exposure to prying eyes. What do you mean by such contradictions?"

With a shrug, he replied, "Even a scoundrel may do the pretty upon occasion."

"I do not see why you felt obliged to follow me, especially after what just passed between us."

"I had to come." His eyes, though half hidden in night and shadow, caught a glow of light.

Looking into those eyes, her confusion strained and faltered. Gradually, as she tried to penetrate the intense look behind the mask, she stepped closer. The meaning of the look was unmistakable.

At last, she smiled. Regardless of what he had said earlier, she knew, he loved her.

It was rare that Miss Cassandra Vickery ever succumbed to an impulse, but she now stood on tiptoe and kissed his lips. She felt him stiffen, freeze, then surrender. His arms went round her so tightly that she gloried in the sensation. After a time, she pulled gently away to gaze at him. The lines of his eyes were tense; his breathing was shallow, his lips a grim line.

"You might as well confess it," she said softly. "You are in as sad a case as I am. You may say what you will to drive me away, but the fact remains, we are both incorrigible."

He held her head to his chest and caressed her hair. "There is something I wish to tell you," he said.

"There is no need. I already know."

Pushing her to arm's length, he said, "You know?"

She replied with a laugh, "I should have to be a perfect dolt not to know that you love me."

"Oh, that."

"Yes, *that*. If you like, you may fall to your knees, shower my hand with kisses and beg me to make you the happiest of men by becoming your bride. I shall not object."

"You like pretty speeches, do you?"

"Oh, yes, and after today, I have grown quite fond of hearing them."

"For myself, I should prefer a little truth."

"Then I shall content myself with hearing you say you love me."

"I shall not bore you by telling you what you already know. Besides, it would be nothing to the point."

"It would be everything to the point." To prove her contention, she kissed him again, and had all the pleasure of discovering that he was incapable of argument when she offered up her lips.

After some time spent in that manner, he wrapped his arms about her and said, "I should like nothing better than to ask you to make me the happiest of men, Cassandra. Unfortunately, I cannot ask for your hand. There are difficulties in the way."

"Oh, do not speak of difficulties. All I wish for is that we may stand here exactly like this forever. That is not a great deal to ask, is it?"

He faced her with a smile. "I should like nothing better than to have the power to grant your wish."

"My dearest wish is to be permitted not to think about Julia or proposals of marriage or anything difficult. What I should like is to go far away, where difficulties cannot follow."

"May I be permitted to accompany you?"

She laughed. "You may accompany me, but only if you do not speak of anything unpleasant."

"And where are we going, if I may ask? To Gretna Green?"

"To London!"

"London?"

"I have never been to London, except to visit the dentist. Surely you recall my telling you as much when we were at Mr. and Mrs. Bumpers's party for Ned."

"Yes, of course. I must have forgotten."

"I expect there is a good deal more to London than the entertainment a dentist can supply."

"Indeed there is: crowds, traffic, noise, air that is thick and grey and malodorous."

"Do not disillusion me. I like to imagine there is dancing, colour, gaiety, prodigies of all kinds and, of course, adventure."

"I suspect this is not the sort of fancy a rector's daughter ought to cherish, my dear Miss Vickery."

"It is exactly the sort she ought to cherish, for it is perfectly safe. You see, there is no likelihood of its ever becoming reality. Therefore, I am at liberty to dream as much as ever I choose."

Under the half-clouded moon, he took her hand and smiled a smile that struck her as rueful. "I believe it is time to say our good-nights," he said.

"So soon?"

"If you do not go now, I shall not be able to let

you go at all, and then the vicar would have himself a dashed apoplexy and you would find yourself in a dashed pickle.''

''Shall we meet again soon?''

''I shall send you a note.''

''Please do not send it by way of Mr. Bradford. I am afraid I should not know how to look him in the eye.''

''No, I would not be so cruel as to send him again with a message to you. Mrs. Clapshew will aid us.'' On that, he kissed her forehead and, with a serious parting look, went toward the gatehouse.

As Cassandra watched the tall, caped figure fade into the darkness, her feelings overflowed, and for once she did not endeavour to quell them. At long last she had received a declaration of love she was not averse to receiving. So full of happiness was she that when she returned to the rectory, tiptoed to her chamber and retired to her bed, she did not once think of what was in store for her on Julia's return or that once again she had forgotten her paintings.

Chapter Eleven

Going Up to Town

While Cassandra slept soundly, smiling as she dreamt, Mr. Bradford caused a dozen candelabra to be brought to his chamber so that he might examine her paintings. He sat for hours, leaning forward over a table spread with pasteboards, endeavouring to determine whether the eleven depictions of the sea nymph were in fact as enchanting as he thought them.

At dawn, when the sun began to shine through his window, he reviewed the pictures. Daylight, instead of dispelling his original impression, confirmed it. Again he was struck by the delicacy and feeling of the paintings, their romantic, adventurous subject, their careful detail, their graceful lines, their humour and charm. Moreover, he perceived that Miss Cassandra Vickery spent many hours in the close study of dragonflies, bumble-bees, roses and bluebells, that the sea nymph was the artist herself, liberated from the confines of a small, quiet country village, that her skill was improving in leaps and bounds with each succeeding picture and that it would improve a thousandfold if she spent a month by the seashore, viewing at her leisure the waves she loved to depict.

Whether an objective eye would concur in his opinions he could not tell. He was so partial to the artist that he might well be blind to her faults. This fact told him, as though he had not known before, how very much in love with her he was.

The upshot of his musings was a determination to go up to Town with the pictures so that he might consult an acquaintance—Mr. Henry Fuseli, who was Keeper of the Royal Academy and an artist whose judgement he respected. He could depend upon Fuseli to render an opinion that was disinterested as well as candid.

Mr. Bradford would have prepared to depart at once but compunction gave him a moment's pause. He did not have Cassandra's permission to show the paintings to anybody. On the contrary, she had been at great pains to keep her pictures hidden from the world. How could he justify laying them before a stranger? How could he knowingly defy her express wishes?

Without putting too fine a point on it, he could

tell himself that he had never actually promised to keep the pictures a secret. At the gatehouse, he had chosen his words carefully, making certain to promise only what he could in truth ensure—that *his cousin* would not see the pictures. He could also recall that the lady herself had at one time confessed that she wished her paintings to be exhibited. By showing them to Fuseli, he was merely helping her achieve her secret ambition.

For some minutes he toyed with these defences, but they did not succeed in convincing him. The fact was that he could not justify himself; therefore, he renounced all attempts. Instead, he waxed philosophical, reflecting that he was in so deep already that it hardly mattered whether he divulged her secret or not. Once Cassandra found out how abysmally he had lied, he would very likely lose any chance of happiness with her. It behooved him, therefore, to bring her work to the attention of Fuseli before that happened.

Mr. Bradford now felt satisfied in regard to Cassandra's paintings. However, he was not satisfied in regard to Cassandra herself. Justifying his continued attachment to her was proving insupportable. It was the height of folly, he had always held, to dangle after a lady whose heart was engaged elsewhere. He was guilty of that very folly every day that he continued to meet with and think about

Cassandra, who loved Marcheek, but instead of extricating himself, he was getting in deeper.

He could justify himself somewhat, he supposed, because it was eminently clear why he loved Cassandra—she was interesting, lively, spirited, feeling, sensible, talented and adorable. What he could not fathom was why she loved Marcheek. Standing at the window of his bedchamber, looking out upon a patchwork of yellow and green fields, he raked his fingers through his hair, trying to understand how it was that a young woman, intelligent and incisive in every other respect, could totally disregard prudence, caution and the threat of scandal for the sake of a bounder. It was vexing, not to say painful, to see his cousin preferred by the one woman he wanted. How could she not know that loving Marcheek would make her the most miserable of creatures, while James Bradford, on the other hand, would exert himself to the utmost in order to make her happy?

And then, as though a sunbeam had poured in through his window to show him the light, he knew the answer. It was so obvious that he wondered he had not seen it before. Love must have blinded him, for ordinarily he was quick to perceive the truth. And the truth was that Cassandra was not in love with Marcheek at all. She had never been in love with Marcheek. She scarcely knew Marcheek, except by reputation, and had talked with him on no more than five or six occasions. Indeed, she had studiously avoided him whenever they were in company, no doubt to oblige her sister and to keep from betraying her supposed affection for him. The only Marcheek she knew, had ever known, was James Bradford. The man she had kissed, the man she had met at the stroke of midnight, the man she had shown her paintings to, the man she really loved, was none other than himself.

He laughed aloud to think that he had been jealous of a phantom. Walking to the glass, he peered into it and declared, ''You have been asleep, you dolt. She loves you. She has loved you all along.''

The gentleman in the glass smiled back at him ironically.

''You are a lucky devil,'' he informed his reflection.

He received a wry nod in return.

''The only difficulty,'' he added, ''is that she does not know it is you she loves and there will be the devil to pay when she finds out.''

When Mr. Bradford set off for London, his spirits were high; despite the difficulties that he knew lay ahead, he was certain that the woman he loved loved him. That was sufficient for the moment to put him in charity with all the world.

He arrived in Bloomsbury in the afternoon and was pleased to find the artist willing to glance at the water-colours. Fuseli asked only two questions—might he perhaps be given leave to study them during the next several days and might he be told the name of the painter? The first question Mr. Bradford answered in the affirmative. As to the second, his response was guarded. He answered only, "The artist wishes to remain anonymous. However, I can tell you that it is a lady." Fuseli continued to press him as to her name and history and was still pressing him when he bade him adieu, promising to return for the paintings in a sennight. Mr. Bradford interpreted this curiosity as a sign that Fuseli had already conceived a certain esteem for the artist. Nevertheless, he parted without giving the slightest hint as to her identity.

As soon as he returned to Cantywell, Mr. Bradford went in search of Mrs. Clapshew. He was pleased to find that she had not yet gone to bed but was busy at her knitting in a cosy parlour, relating the day's gossip to the marquess, who slept peacefully with his head lolling against the back of the chair and an orange striped puss dozing in his lap. Mrs. Clapshew looked up when he entered and, seeing who had come in, assumed the disapproving air she reserved for her employer's nephews.

He set a large box down at her feet and drew up a chair. "How do you do, my dear Mrs. Clapshew?" he enquired solicitously.

"None of your flummery, sir," she sniffed. "All the sugar in the Indies will not make a scallywag anything other than a scallywag."

"As always, Mrs. Clapshew, you are wise and just."

"If you mean to curry favour by agreeing with me, you may as well save your breath."

"I would not think of currying favour, dear lady. Your disapproval is quite precious to me. But it does not deceive me. I know that you are excessively fond of me."

"Butter me up, will you? You mean to ask a favour, I vow."

"Well, in point of fact I do. I should like you to bring a message to Miss Cassandra."

"I guessed as much," she said, masking her gratification.

"I ask that you go and see her in the morning, for I should like her to prepare for a journey tomorrow night. And I should like you to be prepared, as well."

"You need not to take my young lady to Gretna Green, sir. I am sure she will be happy to be married by special license."

He regarded her with amusement. "I am not planning an elopement, dear lady. We are only going to London."

She sat bolt upright so that her knitting tumbled from her lap. While Mr. Bradford went down on one knee and gallantly gathered up the yarn, she cried, "Do you dare take my young lady to London in the middle of the night?"

Having returned the knitting to its owner, he seated himself once more. "I'm afraid we must start our journey considerably earlier than the middle of the night, for you see, if I am to have Miss Cassandra back at the rectory before morning, we ought to set forth just after dark."

"This is madness. You cannot carry her off to London. She will be greatly offended if you do. She will not so much as speak to you forever after."

"On the contrary, she will be enchanted."

"Well, *I* shall not be enchanted, and what is more, I refuse to have any part in it. Now what have you to say to that?"

"Simply this: that my sole reason for arranging the journey is to please Miss Vickery."

"She would never be so wicked as to be pleased with such a scheme."

"Ah, but you see, I know Miss Cassandra. I know her fondest hopes and wishes, and I know that nothing would delight her more than an adventure such as the one I mean to treat her to."

"*Faugh!* You are speaking of Miss Julia Vickery, not Miss Cassandra."

"In spite of appearances, the two sisters resemble each other quite closely in that regard. Miss

Cassandra's imagination conjures up the most exquisite adventures, and I mean to see that one of them becomes reality tomorrow night.''

Mrs. Clapshew had been disappointed in her hopes for a wedding and was not about to encourage a mere flirtation. ''If you are wise,'' she said, ''you will give up this London scheme and tell her that you have been hoaxing her. If you do not, I can tell you all your ruses will be for naught, for I shall not hesitate to tell her myself that you are Mr. Bradford. Then you will be sorry you ever did her such a rascally turn. Miss Cassandra may have one or two romantical notions—all young girls are wont to have their fancies—but she is too principled to wink at boldfaced lies.''

''Mrs. Clapshew, the instant we return from London, I shall unmask myself to her. I wish her to know the whole truth, I promise you, but not before I have had the opportunity to show her an evening she will remember the rest of her life.''

As the housekeeper considered the situation, it occurred to her that a romantic adventure in Town might be the perfect prelude to a proposal of marriage. Thus, she replied, ''If it is to be London, I suppose I shall have to arm myself with a good deal more than a single sack of flour.''

''Then you will accompany us?''

''If I do not look after the poor girl, I do not know who will.''

"You are very kind."

"My intention is not to be kind. I mean to be certain that no harm comes to the child. She is already head over ears in love with you. Heaven knows what might befall if I permitted you to go off with her alone."

"Exactly so. You would never forgive yourself."

"But, Mr. Bradford, you must promise that you honestly mean to tell her the truth afterwards, and that this journey will be the last of these secret meetings and prowlings about the county in masks and such nonsense."

"I do promise. I would gladly pledge my word as a gentleman, but I suspect that would not reassure you greatly."

"It certainly would not!"

"Then I shall simply ask you whether I have kept my word thus far in our dealings."

She shifted in her chair and grudgingly allowed, "I suppose you have."

"Good, then I have one more favour to ask of you. Will you do me the honour of opening this box I have brought you?"

For a time, she eyed him suspiciously. Then, reaching down, she lifted the top off the box and, pushing aside the wrapping, uncovered a resplendent green silk bonnet with a snowy-white plume. She gasped and started back.

Seeing her astonishment, he lifted the hat from the box and handed it to her. "Will you do me the honour of accepting this bonnet, Mrs. Clapshew? I know it is little enough to repay you for your kindness to Miss Cassandra and your endurance of my wicked schemes, but the instant I set eyes on it, I knew it could belong to no other personage than yourself. It would please me greatly if you would wear it."

At first she hesitated, wavering between temptation and the habit of disapproval. He waited patiently until she took the hat in her hands. After a considerable time, she brought it to her head and fitted it on. Looking grim all the while, she tied the ribbon under her chin.

Mr. Bradford stood to admire the effect. He smiled to see the housekeeper rendered speechless by the gift.

At that moment, the old marquess awoke. "What is that you say about the butcher, Mrs. Clapshew?" he murmured. His eyes fluttered open as he became aware of his surroundings. At last they fell on the housekeeper. He blinked rapidly, after which his eyes bulged. Sitting suddenly tall in his chair, he said, "By my stars, Mrs. Clapshew, I have never seen you look so splendid!"

On the day after her meeting with the masked gentleman, Cassandra waited on pins and needles,

anticipating a message from him. Regardless of
who visited her—whether it was Ned Bumpers to
wag his chin at her and throw out veiled hints regarding marriage, or her father to wag his finger at
her and throw out veiled hints regarding spinster-
hood—she did not hear a word that was said, so
eager was she to hear when she would next meet
Lord Marcheek. Her head buzzed with images of
their last meeting, and most especially the moment
when he had confessed he loved her. Though he
had not told her in so many words, his kisses had
spoken eloquently all that she wished to know.

    Her joy could not be complete, however.
Thoughts of Julia marred it. She had not written to
her sister; nor had she paid a visit to Sparrowdene
in order to make her confession. History had taught
her that Julia felt obliged to receive unhappy an-
nouncements with hysterics. It would not do to
have her fill Lady Monck's house with shrieks and
threats. No, Cassandra must wait until Julia returned to Pilkingdown, and then she must tell everything and take her medicine, which, she knew,
would be bitter. Not only would Julia count her as
an enemy, but her parents would be shocked at her
conduct. And unfortunately, Cassandra had no defence. She had behaved badly, every jot as badly
as she had tried to persuade Julia not to behave,
and there was no excuse, no apology that could
mitigate her culpability. The worst of it was that

whenever she thought of Lord Marcheek's soft-
ness, solicitude and affection, she could not bring
herself to feel as remorseful as she knew she ought.

The following morning, while she was in the
kitchen assisting with the jamming, she was interrupted by the sudden appearance of her littlest
brothers and sister, who leapt and clapped their
hands and cried out at the top of their voices that
Mrs. Clapshew had come to Pilkingdown and that
she wore on her head a green silk bonnet, which
Mama declared had certainly been fashioned by
one of the finest London modistes. Hopeful that
the housekeeper had come with a message for her,
Cassandra felt her pulse pound. After wiping her
hands and removing her apron, she went anxiously
to the parlour to greet the visitor. Mrs. Vickery
stayed some time to chat and to lavish many compliments upon the new bonnet, but at long last she
was called away and the housekeeper found an opportunity to speak with Cassandra alone.

In a hurried whisper, she said, "It is to be tonight."

"So soon?" Cassandra answered, delighted.

"You must wear something very fine, my dear."

"I shall wear the brown silk I wear to church."

"No, no—that will not do at all."

"Then the gown I wore to the Cantywell ball."

"Yes, and your mask."

"I should not think of forgetting my mask."

"You are to be ready by nightfall."

"So early?"

"The gentleman would have preferred to meet at the stroke of midnight, as he knows you are partial to that hour, but it is quite out of the question. Moreover, you must not come to the copse but to the gatehouse."

"Ah, we are to meet again at the cosy little gatehouse."

"No, a carriage will meet you there."

"A carriage? But why, Mrs. Clapshew? Where are we going?"

"I cannot tell you. It is to be a surprise."

Cassandra hugged herself. "A surprise!"

"I hope you like surprises, my dear."

"I like them above anything."

"Well, that is good, as you are likely to have your fill of them tonight."

Cassandra had not waited long at the gatehouse when she heard the sound of snorting horses and racing wheels. As the carriage came into view, a door opened and a figure descended. He wore a domino and a mask of white satin. With a sweep of his hand, he bowed and kissed her hand.

"Where are we going?" she asked a little breathlessly.

"To a place where the whole world is masked."

"I never heard of such a place. It cannot be very respectable."

"It has been known to be quite daring, but you will see for yourself in approximately two hours, if we do not dally." He offered his arm. When he saw her hesitate, he asked, "Do you wish to change your mind?"

The carriage stood in silhouette against the darkening sky. It was the same carriage that had sent her and Julia into the ditch many weeks before. That day now formed part of a twilight memory, one that was dim and inconsequential compared to the splendour of the present moment. She looked up to see whether the driver was observing them. He stared straight ahead, as though deaf to anything but the restlessness of the four chestnuts under his command. Neither footman nor tiger could be seen anywhere. Assured of complete privacy, Cassandra inhaled, contained her excitement and allowed him to assist her into the carriage.

Inside sat Mrs. Clapshew wearing her green silk bonnet, a patterned gown of green and yellow and an ample shawl. As Cassandra entered, the housekeeper looked up from her knitting to say, "Do not be afraid, child. Nothing is amiss, and nothing shall be amiss."

Cassandra smiled affectionately. "I am not afraid."

"Oh," Mrs. Clapshew replied, obviously disappointed.

As soon as Cassandra was seated, the gentleman entered and sat beside her. He offered her a rug and a fur, in case the summer night gave her a chill.

"Some of us are a great deal too warm as it is," the housekeeper declared darkly. "A bit of a bracing chill would do some of us a world of good."

Smiling, the gentleman said, "By 'some of us' you no doubt refer to me. I begin to think you disapprove of me, Mrs. Clapshew."

The carriage lurched as the horses were set to at a rapid speed. Steadying herself, Mrs. Clapshew reported, "Do not think to win me with your brazen talk. You are a flirt, sir."

He laughed. "And you like it."

"I do no such thing!"

"Well, if you will not confess to liking me, you will at least confess to liking my taste in hats."

Cassandra smiled. It had gratified her to learn that the gorgeous silk bonnet had come from Lord Marcheek, warmed her to know that he was capable of such graceful generosity. She gave him an eager smile, which he returned in equal measure. They continued to smile at each other until Mrs. Clapshew cleared her throat with the violence of a cloudburst.

To find an object for her eyes other than his

lordship, Cassandra pulled aside the curtain. Perhaps, she thought, she might see one or two points of interest along the road. She gazed for some time; unfortunately, the moon had not yet risen and all she could see was pitch-dark. Letting go the curtain, she sat back and recollected that she did not know where she was going or for how long or what she would find when she got there. Sighing, she gave herself up to all the pleasure of the mystery.

A curious noise roused her from her musings. Mrs. Clapshew had fallen asleep with her chins in her bosom. From time to time, she emitted a snore. Cassandra looked at her companion, who put a finger to his lips and gently collected the knitting which threatened to fall from the housekeeper's lap at the next jolt of the carriage.

He placed the yarn and needles by Mrs. Clapshew's side. "There is nothing like the lulling jounce of a carriage," he whispered, "to send one off in a doze."

"I have never felt more awake," she answered.

His expression told her how welcome this news was. She felt the full force of his attractive smile.

"How shall we entertain ourselves on the journey?" he asked.

"Well, I suppose we might play at Crambo."

"Crambo?"

"My sisters and brothers always like to play

rhyming games whenever we are obliged to take a long journey. But if you do not like to play, we may choose some other game. What would you like best?''

"What would I like best?'' he repeated. After a silence of considerable length, which, judging by his expression, Cassandra felt might well be a prelude to a kiss, he took her hand in his and put it against his cheek. Then, evidently thinking better of the kiss, he let her hand go and shook his head. "I have no objection to Crambo. Indeed, it seems a safe means of passing the time.''

"Safe?''

"*Waif,*'' he said.

"I do not understand.''

"*Waif.* It rhymes with *safe.*''

"No, you misunderstand. I wished to know why you said it was a 'safe way to pass the time.' I should have thought that safety was a subject which interested you not at all.''

"Dash it all, did I say *safe?* I am sure I meant *delightful.* Nothing is so dashed delightful as being confined in a carriage for two hours with a lady one adores and racking one's brains for a dashed rhyme.''

She smiled. "Adores?''

"Now, that is much easier than *safe.* Let me see, there is *floors, shores, roars, bores, chores, sores, snores, gores, carnivores.* The list is endless.''

"Did you just confess that you adore me?"

"Dash it, it is not your turn. I gave you a thousand perfectly excellent rhymes. Now you must give me one. My word is *glove.*"

"My answer is *love.*"

"I have been too easy on you. What can you do with *moneylender?*"

"I can think only of *tender.*"

"*Toe.*"

"*Beau.*"

"*Fashion.*"

"*Passion.*"

"*Liar.*"

"*Desire.*"

"*Sing.*"

"*Wedding ring.*"

He put up a hand. "No more."

"*Adore.* I am aware that we used it earlier, but I cannot think of anything else."

"Are you aware that all your words tend to the same subject?" he enquired.

"Are you aware that yours tend to avoid it? I cannot help wondering why."

"I'm dashed if it ain't obvious. We cannot sit here and speak of love and the like with Mrs. Clapshew snoring in our ears. It would not only be noisy; it would also be imprudent."

"Is our travelling together in this manner prudent? Have our midnight meetings been prudent, or our appearing in masks?''

''No, but I am not the sort of man who would take advantage of Mrs. Clapshew's unconscious state to make pretty speeches to you.''

Puzzled, Cassandra paused. ''You amaze me. That is exactly the sort of man I understood you to be. It is well known you are a favourite with the ladies, and when it comes to taking advantage of an opportunity for intrigue or pretty speeches, you are said to be a complete hand. Yet to me you speak of prudence. What do these contradictions mean, my lord?''

''What contradictions? There are no dashed contradictions. At our last meeting, I made a pretty speech. I said I loved you, did I not?''

''Not precisely. I believe it was *I* who said that you loved me.''

''Well, I agreed with you.''

''That is not the same thing.''

Soothingly, he hastened to reassure her. ''Do not distress yourself over what you imagine to be contradictions. It is quite true I am not myself whenever I find myself in your company, but I assure you, I am perfectly able to make pretty speeches if I put my mind to it.''

Cassandra was alarmed to think that Marcheek, a known flirt, had to put his mind to the task of whispering endearments to her. If that was the case, then perhaps he did not find her as inspiring an object as the ladies who had enabled him to make his reputation. Wounded, she replied, ''I had heard you were so well practised in the art of love-making that it was second nature to you.''

''Yes, but not under these dashed circumstances.''

''I do not think it is the circumstances that inhibit you, my lord.'' Her voice quavered as she spoke. ''I think it is the lady. It is true you are a different man in my company—you find yourself making declarations you later regret. Now you wish to avoid saying more. Nay, you wish to unsay what has already been said.'' Near tears, she looked down at her hands.

''You could not be more wrong, Cassandra. And I shall prove it. But you must be silent. If I am to make pretty speeches to you, I cannot have my concentration disturbed.''

He took both her hands in his and held them to his breast. Reluctantly, she looked him full in the face, still doubting. He closed his eyes and intoned, ''When in disgrace with fortune and men's eyes, I compare thee to a summer's day. Therefore, let us go and catch a falling star and gather our rosebuds while we may, for thy sweet love remembered such wealth brings, that I wonder how I contrive to say such clever things.''

Cassandra laughed, too delighted with his wit to

wonder any longer about contradictions. "Oh, do not stop, my lord. I tremble at your words. I must have more."

"Ah, the lady wants more. Well, more she shall have!" He planted a smacking kiss on her wrist and declaimed, "Men have died and worms have eaten 'em, but not for love."

"Oh, that is very pretty, indeed! The poets must be vastly pleased to hear you take such liberties with their verses."

"Silence," he commanded. He kissed the inside of her elbow, which tickled and made her laugh, and, drawing close so that his lips were a breath from her ear, said, "Let me not to the marriage of true minds admit impediments, for although your eyes are nothing like the sun, you are like a red, red rose, and if we had world enough and time, I would surely produce a dashed rhyme. Therefore, drink to me only with thine eyes and be so good as to come live with me and be my love—" and here he stopped, for he caught sight of Mrs. Clapshew, whose eyes had come close to his and now glared at him with menace.

Chapter Twelve

The Ladies de la Bellebonnette

A rearrangement took place which placed Mrs. Clapshew at Cassandra's side and the gentleman opposite them both. The housekeeper judged that he would sooner be brought to declare himself if his path were not entirely smooth. Nothing forwarded the course of true love so much, she knew, as bitter obstacles.

Meanwhile, Cassandra peeked out the curtains from time to time until, at last, she saw a glow appear in the distance, an arc of brightness against the night-time sky such as she had never witnessed. It seemed to invite her to a land that was not quite real, a land that defied the night and everything that was not brilliant and luminous. Traffic on the road increased and a hubbub surrounded the carriage. Meanwhile, the glow grew larger, encompassing more and more of the sky. At last, she ventured to ask, ''What is that?''

Her two companions looked out the window.

''It is London,'' the gentleman told her with a smile.

She clasped her hands together and put them to her lips. Her eyes filled with tears of pleasure. ''London!'' was all she said.

''You had better keep mum to your sister,'' Mrs. Clapshew advised. ''She will be so envious that she will scratch out your eyes.''

''I have never been to London except to visit the dentist,'' Cassandra said.

The gentleman nodded. ''So I have been told. I devoutly hope this evening will offer something more to your liking than a toothache.''

When the carriage pulled to a stop, the gentleman stepped out to deliver instructions to the coachman. Then the ladies were helped from the carriage, and Cassandra found herself at the head of a flight of stone steps. Her ears were instantly assailed by the din of traffic and the cries of hawkers. Nearby loomed a great flat bridge supported by graceful arches. All was lit by a glow of gas lamps, lanterns and torches. These were reflected in the water which lay at the bottom of the stairs. In the water were barges and wherries of all sizes. Everywhere were men and women of various dress and degree, laughing and calling to one another and sending up sounds of gaiety to mingle with the noises of the city. Cassandra took it all in and, inhaling, lent herself to the sensations that washed over her like a star shower.

Meanwhile, Mrs. Clapshew observed the scene, screwed up her nose and delivered herself of the opinion that "There is a vile stink in the air."

With a lady on each arm, the gentleman descended the steps. In another moment, he led them to a wherry in which sat two burly oarsmen and a boy playing on the French horn. As Cassandra was assisted into the boat, she caught up her skirt in her hand. That immediately attracted the attention of the gallants who hung about the place. They ogled the young lady's shapely stockinged calf until Mrs. Clapshew chased them off by demanding to know what they meant by such looks, and when they told her, not sparing any colour in their description, she shook her fists under their noses.

"What is the matter?" Cassandra asked when the housekeeper was comfortably ensconced beside her in the boat.

"I will not have a parcel of ugly fellows leering at you, my child."

"They were looking at me?"

"I am sorry to say they were. If they would pay half as much attention to the sermons they hear on Sunday, they would profit greatly, I daresay."

"Why do you suppose they were looking at me?"

Mrs. Clapshew, finding herself at a loss to answer, looked to the gentleman to assist her, and found him smiling in amusement.

Seeing the housekeeper's consternation, he fixed an expression of gravity to his lips and said, "They ogle you because they are oglers and that is what they do. They ogle every beautiful creature who comes this way."

"Do they think I am beautiful?"

"If they have their wits, they do."

Cassandra inhaled. She was wholly unaccustomed to being thought beautiful and was endeavouring to believe what she had just heard when her attention was summoned and a goblet handed to her. The gentleman uncorked a bottle and filled her glass.

"What is that?" Mrs. Clapshew demanded.

"Citron," he replied and filled her glass to the top. He removed two handkerchiefs from his sleeve so that the ladies might protect their necks against the breeze.

Sighing happily, Cassandra drank in as many impressions as she could along with the citron.

"Do you like it?" the gentleman enquired softly.

"Very much. It is as if we were so many elves sailing off in a nutshell."

"I should not be the least surprised," Mrs. Clapshew put in, "if we all drowned."

They arrived across the water at another set of stairs. The landing was so crowded with wherries and barges that they bumped one another, so that Mrs. Clapshew nearly fell into the water as she was helped from the boat. Happily, she only fell on top of a portly gentleman who stood on the pier and seemed greatly flattered to find himself lying under so handsome a lady. With great gallantry, he helped her to her feet, but when he expressed the fond hope that he might have the pleasure of another such meeting very soon, she gave him a severe scold and informed him that he ought to know better than to conduct himself like a fribble.

"Where in heaven are we?" she demanded of their escort.

"Welcome to Vauxhall," he said with a bow.

She scowled at the crowd rushing along the stairs. "Why is everyone masked?"

"Possibly because there is a masquerade tonight."

"A masquerade?" Cassandra cried in delighted surprise. "How enchanting."

Mrs. Clapshew said ominously, "No good ever came of a masquerade."

To which the gentleman replied, "Perhaps not,

but there are occasions when a masquerade is a dashed convenient thing.''

As they strolled the Grand Walk, Cassandra took in every picturesque sight that met her eye: the canopy above, the Holland brick beneath her feet, the lofty trees, the statuary, and the lamps, which cast a ravishing display of radiance and shadow. She delighted in it all, especially the costumes of the patrons, dressed as shepherds and shepherdesses, Highlanders, Venetians, abbesses, clowns, huntsmen and sailors.

While Cassandra admired, Mrs. Clapshew delivered her opinion on each costumed figure they passed. She pronounced the men either pickpockets or fops and had not a single kind word for the ladies, whom, she vowed, were not ladies at all. ''That one, for example,'' she said, indicating a tall creature who was dressed in a flowing Grecian costume and was surrounded by a large party of gentlemen. ''I declare, she is no better than she should be.''

''What do you mean?'' Cassandra asked, looking round.

''I mean that she is a pretty piece of baggage and I forbid you to look at her. She is not wearing stays.''

''She looks exceedingly elegant to me.''

''That is because you know nothing of the

world, my child. The creature is a doxy, and the sooner we quit this wicked place, the better I shall like it.''

At that moment, the lady in the Grecian dress looked their way and cried out in rapture, ''Oh, Jamie, is it you?''

Abruptly, the gentleman stopped.

The lady bore down on him. ''Jamie Bradford, it is you or I mistake myself.''

Clearing his throat, he replied, ''Dash it, Lizzie, don't you know me? It is Marcheek.''

''Oh,'' said the lady, crestfallen. ''You looked so handsome I felt sure you were your cousin.''

He smiled. ''I shall not tell him you said so. He will grow so dashed conceited that there will be no enduring him.''

''You are conceited enough for two,'' snapped the lady. Then, rapping him on the breast with her fan, she said, ''You are vilely uncivil, you cox-comb. You have not introduced your compan-ions.''

As he had no choice but to comply, he said, indicating Mrs. Clapshew, ''My lady, may I pres-ent Madam de la Bellebonnette, lately come to live here from France. She speaks not a word of En-glish.'' He winked at the housekeeper, who scowled at him. ''Madame,'' he said to Mrs. Clap-shew as though she were deaf as well as French, ''Lady Foxhill.''

The Countess of Foxhill said, with another fan rap to his breast, "Tell her for me that she is welcome to England, poor thing, and that she is quite safe now. We have no loathsome little corporals here to wreak havoc with the natural distinctions between the lower and upper orders."

He pretended to whisper the translation in Mrs. Clapshew's ear, and though the housekeeper looked daggers at him, he said to the countess, "She thanks you with all her heart."

"And who is this lovely creature?"

"May I present Madame's granddaughter, Mademoiselle de la Bellebonnette."

"Why you certainly may. She is charming. Does she speak English?"

He exchanged a look with Cassandra, who did her best to contain her laughter. "It is quite possible," he said.

"Bon soir," Cassandra said with a modest curtsy. As she rose, she cast the gentleman a mischievous look. *"Je suis enchantée de faire votre connaissance."*

"She is speaking French, I suppose. Nevertheless, she is a sweet puss," the countess declared. "I shall take her and her poor grandmama under my wing."

"That is not necessary, Lizzie," the gentleman hastened to assure her. "I have determined to show them Vauxhall myself."

"And a shocking business you have made of it thus far. Why, they are scarcely dressed for a ridotto. Madame has no mask at all, and mademoiselle has nothing but this pitiful peacock affair to hide her eyes. For shame, Marcheek." In a loud voice, she informed the members of her party that they were to follow her. She then turned to Cassandra to whisper, "La, they bore me to extinction. You are exactly the amusement I require. Now, my dear, we shall go and see the Cascade. Oh, but we must hurry. It begins very soon, and I shall not forgive Marcheek if we miss it. Come along."

Mrs. Clapshew grasped Cassandra's arm and, with a look of horror and a shake of the head, hinted that she must decline.

Cassandra smiled brightly and exclaimed, *"Une cascade! C'est merveilleux, Grandmaman! Allons-y! Vite!"*

They made their way through a crush to a large screen on which was painted a landscape. Though pleasant enough, it did not, to Cassandra's mind, represent anything nearly resembling a cascade. Suddenly, to her pleasure and that of the gasping of the crowd, the landscape was drawn up and there lay revealed the most charming scene: a mountainous view with palm trees and a rainbow. Gurgling through it all was an actual waterfall which flowed from a rock along a declivity and which looked for all the world exactly as though nature had put it there.

"I hope it pleases you, my puss," the countess whispered.

"It is famous!" Cassandra blurted out. "I have never set eyes on anything so ripping."

The countess regarded her with raised brows and observed to the gentleman, "Her English improves rapidly."

"She is a quick study," he remarked.

"Well, enough of that," pronounced the countess after the painted screen had been lowered and the Cascade could no longer be seen. Along with the rest of the crowd, they moved to go. The countess herded them in the direction of the temples.

"You shall dine with us," the countess informed them all, and, accordingly, they were soon installed in a supper-box, from which vantage point they could witness the antics of a juggler and an acrobat. The countess entertained the ladies de la Bellebonnette with a stream of conversation, pausing only to observe *sotto voce* to the gentleman in the white satin mask, "Nothing is so charming as talking with others who merely listen."

Mrs. Clapshew, whose silence had been frosty and sullen up to now, softened her expression when the waiters arrived carrying a chicken, a dish of ham, a dish of beef, a salad, bread, butter, cheese, tarts, custard and a bowl of arrack punch. Because she was unable to talk, she set about supping. So great was her relish as she ate that the gentlemen of the countess's party watched her in admiration. Seeing that her chaperon was happily occupied, Cassandra was at liberty to enjoy herself completely, which she proceeded to do. Never in her life had she seen so much animation, so much colour and lavishness and merriment. She did not think her enjoyment could possibly be greater, but was soon proved wrong when her escort, smiling beneath his white satin mask, asked if he might have the honour of a dance.

Archly, she accepted in French, then rose and placed her hand on his arm. He led her out of the box and they walked along a line of stately tulip trees until interrupted by the appearance of a brightly costumed minstrel, who serenaded Cassandra with a charming variety of French, German and Italian airs. When he had bowed himself off and they resumed their walk, the gentleman said to Cassandra, "I hope you do not mind my giving you French blood and a French name. I thought it would be best if the countess did not know who you are."

Cassandra smiled. "I do not mind at all. It was the liveliest thing to play the role of a mademoiselle."

"I have noticed you are fond of masquerades."

"How quick-witted you are to have thought of such a ruse," she said. "I had no notion you were such an accomplished liar."

The gentleman was not so pleased to receive this compliment as Cassandra was to bestow it. Luckily, conversation was brought to an abrupt end, for they arrived at the juncture of the Grand Walk and Cross Walk where stood the Ballroom, a pavilion which enchanted Cassandra with its magnitude, splendour and fanciful ornaments. She admired the walls painted with representations of Arcadian youths, the Ionic columns decorated with wreaths of flowers, the ceiling coloured to look like the sky and the mirrors shining from every direction.

Smiling at his companion's exclamations of delight, the gentleman led her towards the dancers. The spirited melodies of country dances filled the hall, so that Cassandra could scarcely hold still. To her pleasure, her escort brought her to the head of the line, and for the next hour, she was free to indulge her pleasure in mazurkas and reels. Although neither of them could say much in the course of the next hour, being too caught up in the energy of the dancing, it warmed Cassandra to see that her partner contrived to speak volumes with the laughter in his eyes.

They had paused, out of breath, to refresh themselves with orgeat at a table, when Mrs. Clapshew approached and insisted that now she had dined, it was time to quit Vauxhall.

"Every gentleman in the countess's party has flirted with me, and not a few coxcombs have made lewd suggestions to my face. It was all I could do to keep my appetite. I do not know how I contrived to finish my supper and drink two glasses of burgundy."

"Oh, we cannot leave," Cassandra said. "The countess says there are to be fireworks."

"And there are paintings to see," said the gentleman. "And a soprano, and a bassoonist. Surely you would not wish to forgo hearing the bassoonist."

"Please," Cassandra gently entreated the housekeeper. "I beg Madame de la Bellebonnette will indulge her granddaughter for just one more hour."

Her smile was so engaging that Mrs. Clapshew was compelled to relent. "Very well," she said, "but I insist on your taking this." On that, she pulled from her bosom a small sack of flour and surreptitiously put it in Cassandra's hand, looking about at the crush to see whether the transaction had been observed. "A lady is not safe in this hothouse of vice."

Laughing, Cassandra said, "You are very dear to concern yourself about my safety, but I believe

I am well protected,'' and here she looked up at the gentleman by her side.

Ominously, Mrs. Clapshew shook her head. ''If the rattles and dandies are so lost to all sense that they flirt with *me*, then there is no telling what indignities they may subject you to.''

Once again, Cassandra looked at the gentleman, who made a staunch effort to look grave. ''As always, Mrs. Clapshew,'' he said, ''you are wise and prudent. Really, it is too bad you do not have another sack of flour, so that I might protect myself as well.''

''As it happens, I do have another,'' said the lady, drawing it from her bosom and planting it in his hand. She waved her fingers in their faces, exhorting them to tuck the weapons away on their persons before they should be noticed. When she was satisfied that the sacks had been well hidden, she announced that they might now set out for the temples to view the paintings.

The first painting that greeted them portrayed a shepherd reclining by a stream and playing on his pipe to lure a pretty shepherdess to his side.

''It is a warning,'' said Mrs. Clapshew, ''to all young ladies.''

''If so,'' said the gentleman, ''it is a painting all young ladies ought to see, for it bears a moral.''

''It would bear a good deal more of a moral,'' said the housekeeper, ''if the shepherdess's neck and shoulders were not so bare. What can her mama be thinking of, to permit the child to go out of doors in such attire?''

''I daresay, the climate is a dashed sight warmer in the picture than it is in England.''

Cassandra heard not a word of this conversation, being engrossed in a study of the painting. Its colour and line struck her as so fine that she felt eager to see the other paintings on display. She walked along the gallery to inspect them, and after a considerable time, came away with a forceful sense of her own inadequacies as an artist. She was feeling quite hopeless about her water-colours when it occurred to her that she had not taken them with her when she had run from the gatehouse the night before. Marcheek had come after her to remind her to take her pictures, but she had gone off and left them behind a second time. Not until this moment had she given them a thought.

Mortified, she hurried to the gentleman and tugged him by the sleeve to summon his attention. When he turned to her, smiling, she blushed. ''I hope you were more mindful than I was at our last meeting,'' she said a little breathlessly. ''I hope you remembered to take my pictures with you to Cantywell.''

He paused before saying, ''Yes, I remembered to take them.''

''Thank heaven. I cannot think what possessed

me to forget them. It is unlike me to be so thought-less.''

''I do not know anything about it, of course, but some might think them dashed pretty pictures.''

''Would you be so kind as to send them to me tomorrow? I should like to have them again as soon as I may.''

He inhaled and said resolutely, ''It will be im-possible for me to send them to you tomorrow.''

''Do you wish me to come for them myself? I shall be glad to do so if you think that is the most prudent course.''

''Your coming yourself would accomplish noth-ing,'' he replied seriously.

''I do not understand. How am I to have them back if you will not send them to me and if you will not allow me to come for them myself?''

He would have answered directly, but the count-ess and her party called to them at that moment. Swooping down on them, the countess rapped the gentleman's breast with her fan, crying, ''There you are, Marcheek! You have carried off these de-lightful ladies so that you might have them all to yourself. You are a selfish toad and I have no opin-ion of you.'' Putting one hand through Mrs. Clap-shew's arm and the other through Cassandra's, she declared, ''We shall be inseparable henceforth. As to the men, we shall have none of them.'' Then she drove with the ladies through the crowd, announcing that they must all hurry to the fireworks gallery.

In her anticipation of the pyrotechnical exhibition, Cassandra thought no more of her paintings. As to Mr. Bradford, he followed the ladies rapt in thought. He was well aware that the next time Cassandra enquired about her pictures, he would not be able to depend on the countess to save him.

It was a weary trio who emerged from the countess's barge onto the steps near Westminster and waved goodbye to their hostess and her merry, noisy party.

"Marcheek, you must call soon and bring Madame and Mademoiselle Bellebonnette with you," the lady commanded from the boat. "Foreigners are so charming. One is bored to extinction by those one already knows." When a gentleman of her party loudly objected to this aspersion on his powers of amusement, she rapped him on the cheek with her fan and gave him a scold.

"Au revoir," Cassandra called, waving gaily.

Mrs. Clapshew deigned to nod a farewell and mutter under her breath that it would take a month's ablutions to cleanse her of that night's frippery.

As they made their way up the stairs, the gentleman asked softly, "Well, Miss Cassandra, did you like it?"

"Yes," she answered without hesitation, "just as you knew I would."

They smiled at each other as they emerged onto the street and, looking round for Mrs. Clapshew, saw to their horror that she had been seized from behind by a burly fellow who clapped one hand over her mouth while the other squeezed her middle. At once, Mr. Bradford moved to help her but was stopped by the sound of Cassandra's muffled screams. Like her chaperon, she had been taken from behind. The ruffian had lifted her off her feet so that she kicked the air and, every so often, her assailant's knees. She also bit him, so that he howled indignantly as he tried to drag her into an alley. Mr. Bradford sprang immediately to rescue her but was prevented from getting very far by two brawny toughs, who stood with arms folded, grinning. He threw them aside and contrived to take several steps towards Cassandra and her attacker before the men grasped his arms. One sent a powerful fist into his abdomen. The other drew blood from his mouth with the crack of a walking stick. Mustering all his strength, he broke free. He was stopped at last by a stunning blow to the head. As he fell to the damp cobbles, he heard Cassandra's voice, crying as though from a great distance, "You have killed him!"

Chapter Thirteen

The Engagement

When she saw that Lord Marcheek had fallen, Cassandra grew frantic and accidentally drove her elbow into her assailant's belly. This proved so effective in confounding the fellow that she repeated it. Her assailant let out a gasp and loosened his hold on her arms. Instantly, she ran towards Marcheek, who lay unconscious. She dared not approach too close, for one of the thieves held him pinned to the cobblestones while the other knelt by him, with the intention, Cassandra had no doubt, of searching for his purse. Before she was aware, her attacker caught her again, turned her round to face him and began to demand her money and jewels. He punctuated his demands with his hands, which flew at her so relentlessly that she could scarcely ward off his blows, though she did contrive once to bite his fingers, which threw him into a fit of howling. One of his flailing attempts succeeded in tearing the bosom of her gown, uncovering a small sack. He pounced upon it with a cry of triumph, "I've found 'er jewels, I 'ave!"

Recognizing the sack of flour Mrs. Clapshew had given her, she said, "You will not find anything worth your while in that!"

"So you say," said the grinning thief, who pushed her to the cobblestones, then tore the string from the sack and pulled it open. His face fell when he peeked inside. He sniffed, took a pinch of the flour between his fingers and bellowed, "What in the bloody devil is this?"

"It is flour," Cassandra informed him with pleasure. Swiftly she rose and, snatching the sack from his hand, flung it so that the flour flew into his eyes. He immediately fell back, crying, "I'm blinded. Ye've blinded me. Yer a witch and a demon and I'll have the Robin Redbreasts after ye, I will. I'll have ye up for an action in the court."

Cassandra did not stay to argue. Seeing that the fellow was occupied with trying to rub the flour from his eyes, she rushed to his lordship, who had by now recovered consciousness sufficiently to be rolling on the ground with his two adversaries, exchanging punishing blows to the nose and chest. Because they moved so quickly and roughly, Cassandra was at a loss as to how to assist. Desperately, she looked about her for an object with which to strike the thieves, but none came to hand. At last, when one of the men stood and leaned back to thrust a fist in Marcheek's face, she leapt onto his back, with her hands clutching his throat. He staggered about in astonished rage.

Cassandra saw Lord Marcheek take advantage of this opportunity to deliver the second thief a thumping blow to the chest, which felled him in a heap. The remaining thief, meanwhile, bore down on his pigeon with a vengeance, carrying Cassandra with him on his back.

"The sack!" Cassandra cried out.

The gentleman's eyes met hers and he smiled. He did not need to be told which sack. At once, he reached into his coat and removed the sack of flour Mrs. Clapshew had given him. With a flourish, he opened it and hurled its contents into the face of his attacker, disabling him utterly and covering him—and his passenger—with a white film.

Cassandra was aware only that Marcheek might be harmed. Letting go of her antagonist, she ran to him and put her hand to his head, asking if he had been hurt.

He adjusted his mask and answered with a burst of laughter. "You are covered with flour," he said, and would have spent several delightful minutes brushing the patches of white from her face and hair, but Mrs. Clapshew's voice reached their ears, alerting them that she was still in danger.

Taking Cassandra's hand, he scanned the street to ascertain where Mrs. Clapshew's voice had come from. Anxiously, they both looked, but they could see little, for the gas lamps were sparse. Meanwhile, their attackers sat on the cobbles, rubbing their eyes and complaining that it was devilishly unfair for a cawker to assault an honest flashcove with a flour sack. Nowhere was Mrs. Clapshew to be seen.

She was, however, heard. Turning round, they saw her emerge from a mews, pushing before her a man covered completely in white, looking like a ghostly apparition. As she drove her captive forward, Mrs. Clapshew treated him to a biting lecture. "I must have taken leave of my senses to come to a place where a man will as soon take a decent woman's life as her purse. If I ever set foot in this devil's den again, I hope they will install me at Bedlam." She gave her prisoner a poke with her finger and pronounced him a brute. "London, indeed! I will have none of it. It is nothing but crime and vice, thanks to the likes of you and your brother knaves."

The fellow wailed that hanging was preferable to being bedevilled by a hateful old crone; however, a series of pokes silenced him and induced him to march smartly.

Cassandra and the gentleman exchanged a smile. "You are not hurt," he said to her.

She shook her head and when she drew close to him, he placed an arm around her shoulder and kissed her forehead.

At that moment, the carriage pulled up.

"Where the deuce have you been?" he demanded of the coachman.

"I saw you wuz being attacked, sir," he answered, "and so I went in search of the police."

At that moment, a contingent from the Thames River Police arrived to take the would-be thieves into custody.

"It's off to prison with ye," announced the chief of the law officers. Then, taking one of the thieves by the collar to lead him away, he screwed up his face and said, "Seems along with runnin' afoul of the law, yev run afoul of the flour bin."

Installed safely inside the carriage, the ladies fell to arranging their persons and assessing their injuries, which happily proved negligible.

Removing his linen from his coat, the gentleman gently brushed flour from Cassandra's cheeks and nose, remarking that she had been amazingly brave during their late adventure. She blushed, revelling in his attentions to her upturned face.

"I thought you had been killed," she said to

him. She touched a bruise that had begun to turn purple on his brow.

"I could not possibly be killed."

"Why not?"

"I cannot be killed until I have said what I have to say to you."

"What do you have to say to me?" asked Cassandra, thinking that the only thing wanting to make this night perfect was a proposal of marriage from the man she loved.

Mrs. Clapshew chose that moment to snatch the linen from his hand and call him a scapegrace and a rapscallion.

He settled back, amused, while the housekeeper did the offices of restoring Cassandra to an unfloured condition.

"It took great courage to subdue that dreadful man," Cassandra said to Mrs. Clapshew in admiration.

"He would have stolen my bonnet," Mrs. Clapshew said indignantly. "I was perfectly civil, promising him my ring and the half crown I carry in my stocking. But would he be satisfied? No, he must have my bonnet, too. He vowed he would get a pretty price for it in the rookeries. I restrained my temper as best I could, but I do not know how it is possible to converse rationally with a goosecap. Nothing could persuade him; he would have my bonnet, he said. And so I was obliged to douse him.'' All at once, she began to sniffle.

Cassandra patted her hand and murmured soothing words.

''Do not weep, Mrs. Clapshew. You did very right to douse him,'' the gentleman said.

The housekeeper answered this assurance with a spasm of sobs. ''I am not a vicious creature, I hope, but he would have taken my bonnet. As it is, he has torn it dreadfully.'' On this, she blew her nose into the floury linen and removed the hat from her head. She had no need to untie it for its ribbon was torn to shreds. The silk was speckled with flour and its snowy-white plume lay limp, like an ailing goose.

Cassandra quickly assayed the damage and declared, ''It is not beyond repair. You may sew a new ribbon on again. It is no work at all to spruce up the rest. I shall assist you, if you like.''

''It will never be restored,'' the housekeeper wailed, weeping in despair.

''If your ministrations do not restore this bonnet,'' said the gentleman, ''I shall return to London and buy you a new one.''

This promise reminded Mrs. Clapshew that it was he who had been to blame in the first place for the damage to her bonnet and her dignity. She therefore scolded him, ''I'll have none of your flummery, sir. You have put my young lady and me in jeopardy such that we might never have come home with our lives and our virtue if I had not thought to bring a bit of flour.''

''Exactly so. And that is why I shall buy you a new hat. You have saved our lives and are a prodigious heroine.''

Mrs. Clapshew pouted at him as he smiled at her. ''I do not wish to be a heroine, and I am perfectly content with the hat I have.''

''You shall have a new one, with my compliments.''

Again, the housekeeper began to weep. ''You must promise me, sir, you will not go back to that vile place, that hellish city, not for a bonnet nor for any other reason. Suppose you were to be killed next time?''

''Why, I do believe you are anxious for my skin,'' he laughed.

''Though you are a snake and a scoundrel,'' the housekeeper declared between sobs, ''you do not deserve to be killed by thieves and villains, and I do have hopes that you may be reformed if you marry prudently.''

''I thank you. I am greatly moved to know that you nurture an affection for me, however minuscule, in your heart of hearts.''

When he kissed her hand and smiled at her, she snorted, ''You are gammoning me, sir.''

"I am certain he means every word," said Cassandra, throwing him a tender look.

In this manner, the time passed quickly until, just as the sun hinted it might turn the sky a deep rosy shade, the carriage drew up at the gatehouse.

Assisting Cassandra to the ground, the gentleman said, "I shall walk with you to the rectory. We may talk as we go."

Cassandra bade the housekeeper goodbye and put her hand on the gentleman's arm. Although the sky was not the London sky, aglow with sparkle and alive with the hum of traffic and crowds, it was silently splendid. A hint of stars could be seen above the ribbon of dawn rising beyond the trees. Inhaling, Cassandra looked up at her escort. Behind his mask, his eyes were grave and intense.

"It is almost morning," she said.

"And therefore, I had better speak quickly."

She nodded. Her pulse pounded as she waited to hear the words which would make her his betrothed.

"I have taken your pictures up to Town," he said.

Cassandra stopped. Apart from the fact that she had not expected him to allude to her paintings, she did not recollect having seen them in the carriage that night and so she could not understand how they could have been taken to London. Puzzled, she regarded him.

"I went up to Town yesterday and took them to an acquaintance who I thought might wish to exhibit them."

Her lips parted and she took a breath. Appalled, she cried, "I thought you knew nothing about such things! I thought you knew I wished them to be private!"

"On the latter point—that I was aware of your wish to keep the paintings secret—you are correct. I knew your sentiments, and I proceeded nevertheless. On the former point, however, I have a confession to make. I do know a trifle about such things, more than just a trifle, in fact." Though it pained him to see her expression of horror, he would have persevered, explaining that he was James Bradford, and not Lord Marcheek, but he was interrupted by the sound of carriage wheels. He had only an instant to pull Cassandra out of harm's way before the conveyance raced noisily past. He followed it with his eyes as it turned in at the gatehouse and disappeared along the approach to Cantywell.

"It is Dr. Suckling's carriage," Cassandra said in alarm.

Briefly, they looked at each other. "Your uncle," Cassandra said. "He is ill."

"If he has sent for the doctor in the middle of the night he is deathly ill, for he never will have the doctor, no matter how bad he is."

"You must go to him at once."

"But I must know if you are angry. Do you blame me for taking your pictures?"

"Yes. No. I do not know."

"I have not told you all." Gently, he took her hand.

Distressed to think that he had another such announcement to make, she murmured, "Dear me, there is more? I have not absorbed all that I have heard thus far. I do not think I can hear more."

"You must hear it, Cassandra."

"Go to your uncle, please. I shall hear everything you have to say in good time." She tried to tear herself from his grip.

"I love you," he said, then let her go.

She neither paused nor answered. All she could think was that her night of adventure and enchantment was over and now she must face the light of day.

She had scarcely an hour to wash the flour from her face and hair, change her clothes and appear in the bakehouse as though she had slept the night away in her own bed. The servant girl was already carrying in bowls of cream and slabs of butter from the dairy when she arrived. In the hurry of mixing batter for gateau, she scarcely had time to think of the astounding news she had lately received from

Lord Marcheek; yet her mind would not fix on anything else.

That he had done precisely what he knew would mortify her struck her as incredible. It sickened and maddened her beyond anything she had known. Then, instead of acknowledging that he had done wrong or that he was sorry, he had declared that he loved her. What was she to think?

She could think only what she had so often thought in regard to Lord Marcheek: that he was full of contradictions. This was one inconsistency, however, that she could not reconcile. How was it possible, she asked herself over and over, for a man to love a woman and betray her so abominably? She whipped the batter with energy, but no answer came.

Instead, Julia came, rushing into the bakehouse in a pucker, full of news of her visit to Sparrowdene and the joys of being far from the dullness of Pilkingdown Rectory.

The sisters embraced, and Julia, her eyes agleam, declared, ''I have come to find you, Cassie, to tell you the news at once.''

''Dear me, more news.'' Her mind leapt to the confession she must make to her sister without further delay.

''I have not told Mama and Papa as yet, for I thought you ought to know it first, as it will affect you most nearly.''

"Is it happy news?"

"It is to me, and it will be to Mama and Papa, but as to you, I do not know." Here, she smiled.

"If it will bring happiness to my family, I shall be happy."

"Will you, indeed?" Julia laughed sceptically. "In that case, you will be happy to know that I am engaged to marry Ned Bumpers." She waited for her sister's reaction.

Cassandra paused. "Ned Bumpers? But you were determined to have Lord Marcheek. You were willing to risk scandal to fix him. How is it possible to change your mind so suddenly?"

"His lordship did not call once while I was at Sparrowdene. Ned visited often and fell head over ears in love with me."

"Julia, did you promise yourself to Ned in order to spite me? I beg you, tell me the truth."

Incensed, Julia shot back, "I should have no objection to spiting you, but in this instance, it is not an incentive. The fact is that his parents have agreed to take a house in Town."

Cassandra put her hand to her forehead and sat down on a stool in utter dejection. The situation could not have been worse, in her view, if she had confessed she was in love with Marcheek and had called Julia's wrath down upon her head. She did not believe her sister would be any more happy

with Ned than she would have been with his lordship.

Julia demanded, "Well, are you going to wish
me happy?"

"How can I? Your misery is assured."

"Oh, you wrong me, Cassandra. You say that
because you are jealous. Though you did not want
Ned for yourself, you do not wish to see anybody
else have him."

Rising, Cassandra pleaded, "Will you recon-
sider? You cannot be happy if you marry a man
merely for his house in Town."

In high dudgeon, Julia protested, "I am doing
no such thing. As it happens, I think Ned is a sweet
old thing and we shall deal famously together. He
worships me and I quite like being worshipped. I
am determined we shall be blissful."

"I would give much to be able to believe you,
but I cannot. I know that you set your cap for Lord
Marcheek purely on account of his house in Town.
It meant more to you than even his title and fortune."

"What do I care for Lord Marcheek?" Julia said
with a shrug. "He is dead, anyway."

Stunned, Cassandra caught her breath. "Dead!"

"You did not know? Evidently, the news has
not reached you here at the rectory as yet. Well,
you shall hear of it soon enough. Lord Marcheek

was killed in a duel last night. His corpse was carried to Cantywell not two hours ago. Much good his house in Town will do him now!''

Chapter Fourteen

Unmasked

Mr. Bradford sat at the bedside, waiting for his cousin to wake. The doctor had removed a single bullet from his shoulder, bled him, bandaged him and assured the fretful marquess and his household that the young earl would be right as rain again in no time. Marcheek now slept peacefully; therefore, his uncle took himself off to do likewise. Although he knew Marcheek was out of danger, Mr. Bradford refused to quit his side until he had heard the history of the wound.

He was about to doze off in the chair when he was startled by a moan and a voice saying, "Dash it, James, I've been kicked in the head by a horse."

"You were shot in the shoulder, not the head," said Mr. Bradford, rousing himself.

"My shoulder be dashed. My head is about to

burst. I ought never to drink blue ruin. It makes mice feet of me. I'll be dashed if I so much as sniff the frog's wine again.''

''What happened to you, Marcheek—apart from your having too much gin, I mean? How the deuce did you contrive to get yourself shot?''

''It was Lord Loveless's doing. He discovered me at The Star and Garter, whether by design or accident I know not. He approached me while I was at Hazard and called me out, proposing a duel with pistols. Naturally, I refused. I was winning, after all. When I declined his invitation, he called me a whey-faced poltroon. I chose to overlook the slight as he was a trifle the worse for drink and as I did not wish to interrupt my game. But he was not having any of my civility. He gave me his glove across the cheek.''

''And so you commenced to duel?''

''Oh, no. You see, I had a notion that if I turned the other cheek, as one is supposed to do, he would go away. I am not at all averse to conducting myself in proper fashion if it will save me from an awkward situation.''

''But he did not go?''

''Oh, yes, he bundled off, mad as hops, and I went back to the table. Unfortunately, I lost all my winnings, and then some. Dash it, coz, I don't suppose you could advance me a little of the ready?''

''Get to the duel, Marcheek.''

"Yes, well, I'd been persuaded to have a taste of max—very good juice, I was assured, and later, feeling a bit foxed, I went out to the stable for a nap. When I arrived, there was Loveless, waiting for me. He carried two pistols and insisted I shoot at him, for he had every intention, he said, of shooting at me."

"Was there a surgeon present? Were there seconds?"

"No. He'd made a havey-cavey business of the thing and I did not hesitate to say so. No wonder, I said, that Lady Loveless had sought solace with a bounder such as myself—her *caro esposo* was a complete bumble. Perhaps I ought not to have alluded to her ladyship just then, for he treated me to the blackest look, placed a pistol in my hand and marked off twenty paces. Then he turned and shot me in the shoulder and demanded that I shoot him, as well. I thought I might as well shoot, for the lobcock was not likely to take himself off until I did, and so I shot him in the foot, which appeared to satisfy him."

"He shall be arrested, of course."

"I doubt as much. He has left England by now. And I do not wish to see any great harm come to him, for I am excessively lucky that he shot me in the shoulder. He was aiming for my head."

"I knew it would come to this one day."

"Well, the entire affair is your fault, James. I hope you are pleased with this night's work."

"*My* fault? Did I not warn you? Did I not caution you to be prudent?"

"*Faugh!* Of what use is that? You ought to have come with me to The Star and Garter. Had you been there, none of this would have happened. You would have quieted Loveless and talked him out of this notion of grass before breakfast. You are entirely to blame, neglecting me for the sake of a filly who does not even know that she ought to love you. However, you may redeem yourself by making me a present of five hundred."

Mr. Bradford rose. "Good night, cousin. I am glad you have not been killed. I am glad neither of us has been killed tonight." He moved to the door.

"Very well, forget the five hundred, James. I shall make do very nicely with three."

But it was too late. Mr. Bradford had gone to tell his uncle that his heir was awake, and as impudent as ever.

"How do you know Lord Marcheek is dead?" Cassandra asked breathlessly.

Julia preened, feeling all the importance of being the bearer of gruesome tidings. "I know because Dr. Suckling was at Sparrowdene last night. He had been called on account of Lady Monck's having a fit of tertian ague. She woke the entire household because she could not sleep, and so the doctor was sent for. Dr. Suckling had just left her bedside when the servant came from Cantywell to say that he had been to Hopcross to seek him and was told he was to be found at Sparrowdene. He had lost more than an hour in seeking him and very much feared his master had fallen off his perch by now. Dr. Suckling asked if Lord Cantywell had had a seizure, whereupon the servant said it was not the marquess who needed attention but Lord Marcheek, though by now he might have better use for a clergyman than a surgeon. Naturally, Dr. Suckling went off at once and I came away just at morning, for Papa had arranged to have Joseph Small bring me in his cart.''

''I do not believe it.''

''The servant said his lordship had been all night at The Star and Garter and had fought a duel.''

''No, no, it is not possible.''

''Why, what do you mean?''

The question stopped Cassandra. She knew that any attempt at an answer was out of the question. Under no circumstances could she reveal to Julia or anybody else that she had spent the previous night in London with Lord Marcheek.

Even if she had been tempted to take her sister into her confidence, she would not have known what to say, for she was altogether confused. The only thing that was clear to her was that a man, even one as charming as Lord Marcheek, could not be in two places at the same time. If he had been at The Star and Garter, he could not have been with her at Vauxhall, and if Lord Marcheek was not with her at Vauxhall, then a man pretending to be Lord Marcheek had been with her, and if a man had impersonated Lord Marcheek with such success, then it was someone who resembled him very closely, a cousin, for example, and if it was a cousin, then she knew now why he was so interested in her paintings and had taken them up to Town without her permission.

For a moment, Cassandra stared at the bowl of batter, overpowered by a sense of her own foolishness. Then, without a word, she ran into the house, seized her bonnet and set out for Cantywell at a run.

When she arrived, out of breath and full of dread as to what she was about to learn, she asked for Mrs. Clapshew. That lady was breakfasting in the kitchen, she was told, and not waiting to be announced, Cassandra made her way belowstairs. The housekeeper sat over a cup of tea by the cook stove, half dozing in the warmth of its fire. She looked up when Cassandra drew out a chair and sat.

"Ah, the vigour of youth," Mrs. Clapshew observed. "You do not appear the least sleepy, my dear. I, on the other hand, can scarce keep my eyes open.'' She rested her head on her hand and closed her eyes.

''There is too much news for sleeping. I have heard that Lord Marcheek has been shot. Is it so?''

Yawning, Mrs. Clapshew replied, ''Yes, and no more than the scallywag deserves.''

''Is it true he is dead?''

''Gracious, no. He is only wounded. Do not tell me the gossips have him buried so soon.'' She rubbed her eyes and endeavoured to blink herself awake.

''Mrs. Clapshew, how can Lord Marcheek have been shot in a duel at The Star and Garter when he was with us in London the entire night?''

The housekeeper opened her mouth as if to explain. Then, as she recollected the nature of the explanation, she turned several shades of pink and looked conscious. Her guilty expression confirmed what Cassandra had suspected.

Cassandra summoned her courage. ''It was not Lord Marcheek who escorted us to London, was it? It was Mr. Bradford.''

Mortified, Mrs. Clapshew nodded.

''And it was not his lordship who met me at the temple and the gatehouse. It was Mr. Bradford, was it not?''

Folding her hands prayerfully, Mrs. Clapshew cried, ''He swore he meant to tell you the truth himself, and he would have done if this accident had not called him away.''

Cassandra put her hands to her face and sighed. ''I cannot bear to think how I permitted myself to be taken in. I believed him completely. I am a silly, romantic fool.'' She did her utmost to resist the tears that started.

''Ah, do not recriminate, my dear. It is not the worst thing in the world to be a silly, romantic fool. We all do it from time to time.''

''You are right, Mrs. Clapshew. It is not the worst thing.'' Her eyes were narrow and her voice ominous. ''It is much worse to be a liar and a cheat!''

The housekeeper's back went straight; her eyes grew wide. She had never before heard such a tone of fierceness in the voice of the rector's daughter. Indeed, nobody ever had.

''Do not be in a pet, child. It is true the gentleman did very wrong, but I believe he loves you.''

''So he has gammoned you, too!''

''Upon my word, nobody gammons me. I speak the truth—he loves you. I only wish I had not been persuaded to help forward his schemes. Now you will blame me and will not come to visit me ever again.''

Cassandra put an affectionate hand on Mrs. Clapshew's. ''Let us not quarrel, old friend. I should be miserable if I could not visit you.''

"Ah, you are a good, forgiving child." She embraced Cassandra and then, letting her go, wiped away tears with her apron.

Cassandra, who had remained perfectly calm, asked, "Will you be so good as to tell Mr. Bradford I wish to meet him tonight?"

The housekeeper sighed. "Yes, I shall. It is best that you let him tell you the truth. And if afterwards you torment him a little for his deception, well, that is what lovers must do, I expect, before they can permit themselves to be happy."

"Please do not tell him that I know everything."

"Certainly not! I know he wished to tell you the whole truth himself. I quite believe it is a point of honour with him."

"Honour, indeed! Please tell him, if you will, that we shall meet at the temple."

"The temple in the copse. I shall tell him. At what hour?"

"At the stroke of midnight, of course."

Everything was as it had been at their first meeting: the stars lit the sky, the night breeze was gentle, Mrs. Clapshew was punctual at the gate, the gentleman wore a mask of white satin. The only difference Cassandra could observe was the change in herself. Instead of anticipation, she felt a blue-hot anger. Instead of abandoning restraints, she knew she must hold her emotions in check. Instead of aching with pleasure when she first set eyes on the man in the mask, it was all she could do to smile cordially and permit him to hand her up the steps of the temple.

He reached to embrace her, but she evaded him gracefully so that he had to content himself with taking both her hands in his and raising them to his lips. She watched closely as he planted a kiss on each of her fingers, which itched to strike him.

"At last," he said, "I can tell you what I've wished to tell you for some time."

"Yes, of course. But first, I have news I must tell you. And not very pleasant news, I fear."

She saw alarm in his eyes. "You are not ill, are you?" he asked. "None of your family are ill?"

"It is Mr. Bradford."

She was pleased to see that she had taken him by surprise.

"What about Mr. Bradford?"

Though her voice shook, she went on, certain that he would mistake her trembling for tender emotion. "My parents pressed me so vigorously on the matter of Ned Bumpers that I was obliged to tell them of Mr. Bradford's offer. Now they wish me to marry him—and as soon as possible, by special license, if it can be arranged." The frown on his face gratified her.

"What did you answer?"

"Of course I answered that I should sooner die than be married to such a boor."

"You think him a boor?"

"Not merely a boor, but an interfering, officious, high-handed, bracket-faced boor. I cannot bear to look at him."

"I see."

"He wears such a self-satisfied smirk that it is punishment to sit in his company."

"I conclude that you find him intolerable in every way."

"Oh, pardon me, I do not mean to offend by speaking ill of your cousin. Naturally, you are prodigiously fond of him. You cannot help it—he is so close to you in every conceivable way."

He let go of her hands. "You know."

"I beg your pardon?"

"You know that you are addressing James Bradford and not his cousin."

Almost breathless with anger, she turned her back on him. "Unlike yourself, Mr. Bradford, I am not an accomplished liar. Yes, I know. I know everything."

"You may think you know everything, but I assure you, you do not. If you did, you would know that I love you. That part was not masquerade. In your heart you know I speak the truth." He took her by the shoulders and compelled her to face him.

She would not meet his eyes. "Please do not presume to speak for me. In my heart I hate you."

"You do not hate me. Quite the opposite. You fell in love with a man in a mask of white satin. That man was, and is, James Bradford, regardless of what he may call himself. Furthermore, he wishes to marry you."

She declined to notice this declaration, which not twenty-four hours earlier would have made her the happiest of women. "Sir, I should like you to return my pictures to me at once."

"You shall have them in five days."

"Five days! I cannot trust them in your care for five days."

"I have promised Mr. Fuseli a week. You shall have them at the end of that time."

Helplessly, she blurted out, "You are the most difficult, conceited, obstinate man I have ever had the misfortune to meet!"

Lounging against a pillar, he replied, "And you are the most interesting, intelligent and delightful woman I have ever had the good fortune to meet."

His refusal to dispute took the wind out of her sails. She paced a moment, aware that he watched her. In heavy silence, she paced for some time, until at last her anger spent itself. Sorrow replaced it, threatening to overwhelm her with anguish. Stopping in her tracks, she met his eyes, which were rendered intensely black by the mask.

In a voice so soft that he knew she was in dead earnest, she said, "You lied to me. I can never forgive that. Nor can I trust you. I can only wish for your absence, for it is painful to look at you."

"Then you shall not be forced to do so any longer," he said grimly. He took her by the waist and kissed her, then pulling himself from her, descended the steps and went away.

Chapter Fifteen

And, after all, what is a lie? 'Tis but
The truth in masquerade.

—Lord Byron

On the following Sunday, the banns were read
for Ned Bumpers and Miss Julia Vickery. Along
with the villagers of Hopcross and the surrounding
county, the Marquess of Cantywell appeared in
church to hear the marriage announced, but he appeared quite alone. His nephews, he reported to his
neighbours with a heavy sigh, had concluded their
visit and gone away. "They are the best lads an
uncle ever entertained," he lamented. "I shall feel
their loss."

The news left everyone completely cast down,
everyone that is except Cassandra, who rejoiced.
Nothing could please her more, she told herself,
than to be able to walk the lanes of the county and

the High Street of the village without danger of
meeting Mr. Bradford. Had he remained in the
neighbourhood, she should have been obliged to
keep indoors for the remainder of the summer
merely in order to avoid him, and she was unwilling to make such a sacrifice when the Queen
Anne's lace was in bloom and ripe for sketching.

At the end of five days, she received a package
containing her water-colours, which she had given
up hoping ever to see again. No note accompanied
the package, no attention of any kind.

She locked the paintings away in their hiding
place. Because they reminded her vividly of how
foolish and romantical she had been, she could not
look at them. She thought often of the gentleman
who had so disillusioned her and acknowledged
that it would be a long while before she would be
able to recollect him without a pang.

The banns had been read three weeks for the
bridal couple when Cassandra received a letter
from Mr. Henry Fuseli:

My dear lady,
Pardon my not addressing you in proper form.
Mr. Bradford will not reveal your name or
your direction. If you receive this letter, it is
because he has been so good as to forward it
to you. Having seen your paintings, I am compelled to write to say how delightful I found

them. They demonstrate a considerable skill, an accurate eye and a charming fancy. I could wish that they were not so small in size or so limited in subject. However, I do wish to advise you that if you persevere in your painting to the extent of producing additional pasteboards, I should like to have a look at them with the object of considering them for exhibition. Mr. Bradford wishes me to assure you that my opinion is in no way influenced by him, as that would be disgusting to you. Yours, etc.,

H. Fuseli

It was some time before Cassandra could be private enough to reread the letter and absorb its contents. Mr. and Mrs. Bumpers and Ned had come to dine, and there was a great uproar as every detail of the imminent wedding was gone over a hundred times. Happily, Pilkingdown Rectory was so old-fashioned as to dine at five. Therefore, at seven, Cassandra had the opportunity to tiptoe to her attic room where she could read alone and undisturbed.

Several perusals of the letter left her head swimming with impressions and emotions. She was both thrilled and humbled to think that a respected artist and curator had taken the trouble to encourage her to persevere in her painting. Evidently, he did not think Marietta and her adventures were either wicked or ridiculous. He had even gone so far as to invite her to submit a full complement of pictures for exhibition. It was incredible, exactly what she had dreamed of, or rather, had been too afraid to dream of.

And for this good fortune, she was aware, she must be grateful to Mr. Bradford, who had ignored her wishes and fears and brought the pictures to Mr. Fuseli's attention. It occurred to her, as she considered what he had done, that his risking her displeasure had demonstrated as nothing else could the depth of his affection for her. What better token of love could he give than to do what he felt was best for her, even though she declared it was the very last thing she wanted?

It was not lost on her, either, that Mr. Bradford had refused to disclose to Fuseli her name and direction. He had taken what pains he could to protect her privacy. Such care indicated that he was not as insensible to her wishes and fears as she had believed.

The final sentence of the letter stung her. Clearly, Mr. Bradford believed that she harboured the blackest resentment against him, and well he might, for she had expressed herself with uncommon passion during their last meeting at the temple. For some years now, she had held it as an article of faith that it was an excellent thing to express oneself passionately, to free oneself from the bonds of pretence and politeness and say all that one wished to say without disguise. That night, she had done it. She had let forth her anger without reserve. To her consternation, she was not satisfied with the result. Indeed, she now felt that in certain instances, passion was not so delightful a sensation as she had anticipated and that there was much to be said for restraint. She had spoken in such a manner as to give Mr. Bradford every reason to believe she would hate him forever. As he had gone from Hampshire, it was now too late to disabuse him.

Not only did she not hate him, but, she acknowledged, she loved him, just as he had said she did. It was possible, she found, to be deeply angry with a man and still wish to be with him every minute of the day and night. Furthermore, she felt certain he was exactly the man to suit her, a man who would not merely take her pictures up to London, but would take *her*, as well, a man who would buy Mrs. Clapshew a bonnet, weave pretty speeches out of the best-known love poems and ask her to marry him despite her lack of fortune and connections. Most of all, he loved her. He had neither disguised nor pretended there. She had felt his love the way she felt enfolding summer breezes. True, he was also the man who had deceived her, but hadn't she deceived Julia? The only difference between them was that she had been somewhat absolved by Julia's engagement.

These thoughts occupied her mind so completely over the next weeks that it required all her resolve to take part in the general merrymaking. Seeing the happiness of Ned and her sister reminded her stingingly of the happiness she had pictured for herself. As the carriage departed the churchyard to carry the honeymoon couple and the groom's parents up to Town, Cassandra sighed with relief. No longer would she be required to rhapsodize and smile. She waved the honeymooners off, looking forward to an hour alone with her tears.

The crowd of well-wishers dispersed. Among them was Mrs. Clapshew. "How do you get on, my dear?" asked the housekeeper with the same heartfelt concern one might bestow on an invalid.

"I am well enough, thank you. I congratulate you on your bonnet. It appears as good as new. Mr. Bradford will not be required to fetch you another from Town."

The housekeeper patted the plume, which had been revived and perched pertly atop the green silk. "Mr. Bradford has better things to do, I'm sure, than fetch me a hat from Town. He is soon to embark on a journey to the other side of the world."

Her face hot, Cassandra asked, "Where do you suppose he means to travel this time?"

"His letter to Lord Cantywell said he had a

fancy to see the Orient again. These rapscallion fellows will never stay in one place, you know.''

''I suppose Hampshire is the dullest place imaginable to such fellows.''

''Is the Orient very far from Hopcross, do you suppose?''

''Yes, very far. I expect he means to go soon.''

''Very likely. He has no reason to put off his departure, now that his scallywag of a cousin has some use of his shoulder again and is in no immediate danger of joining the devil's ranks before his time. I daresay, the sooner Mr. Bradford can put a distance between himself and his conscience, the better he will like it.''

''His conscience?''

Mrs. Clapshew waxed irate. ''It is not merely a question of his lying to you. It is a question of his breaking your heart—the sweetest child who ever was dandled on a knee, a good and gentle and kind young miss who would never think to trick a fellow creature as she was tricked. I confess, I cherished the hope he would marry you and make it up to you, but as he did not, I gave him a wigging he shall not soon forget.''

''Oh, dear. I hope you did not tell him he broke my heart. It makes me sound so pitiful.''

''I warned him at the outset there would be the devil to pay if he did not confess the truth straightaway. But would he heed me? Of course not. He would put it off and put it off and say he must first take you up to London and such nonsense. And you see the result—both your hearts dashed to pieces. He ought never to have taken you to that sink of corruption.''

Earnestly, Cassandra said, ''I am glad he took me to London. I shall never forget it. My only regret is that I never thanked him.''

''Thanked him? My dear, I begin to think you still nurture a bit of a tendre there.'' Mrs. Clapshew studied her face.

Cassandra could not think of a reply that was not painful. Therefore, she said, ''Well, good day to you, Mrs. Clapshew.''

The housekeeper would not permit her to go. ''Stay one moment, if you will. I have been asked to deliver this note.'' Smiling slyly, she handed Cassandra a paper.

For a moment, Cassandra stared, whereupon Mrs. Clapshew flapped a hand in her face and snapped, ''You always knew what to do with one of these pieces of tomfoolery before. You are to open it and read it.''

Incredulous, Cassandra unfolded the note. It contained no salutation, no signature, simply the words—

Be so good as to meet me tonight. You know the place and the hour.

* * *

The night was so cold and wet that Cassandra wished she had taken an umbrella. She had not gone two yards before her boots were thick with mud. The wind came up and drove the rain into her face, drenching her cloak. If she had not known the route so well, she might have been in danger of losing her way. As it was, she arrived at the gate at the same time as Mrs. Clapshew, who bundled Cassandra under her umbrella and muttered imprecations against the foul weather.

"You have only to call if you should need me," she whispered as she deposited Cassandra near the steps of the temple.

"I thank you," Cassandra answered, trying to discern a masculine figure amongst the pillars, the rain and the darkness.

When at last she did see him, lounging in the shadow of a Doric column, she was surprised to observe that in addition to wearing his cloak and sombrero, he was masked. What was the point of disguise now, she wondered.

His arms were folded; he waited for her to ascend the steps.

When she approached, he greeted her cordially. "I congratulate you on the good fortune of your family," he said. "I trust your sister and her bridegroom will know every happiness."

She made no reply. Unlike him, she could not pretend to lightness of heart.

He stood away from the column and took a step closer. With an abrupt gesture, he removed his hat, then his mask. Even in the shadow, she could see that his face was taut and she wished she might touch it.

After a click of the heels and a smart bow, he said, ''I believe we have been introduced in form, but permit me to present myself again—James Bradford. I am at your service.'' He waited, unmoving, to see whether she would run away or retort in anger.

For some time, she alternated between glancing at the mask in his hand and his grave expression. At last, having resolved to convey to him somehow her true feelings, she dipped a curtsy. ''I am pleased to make your acquaintance, Mr. Bradford,'' she said. She could see that he had not expected such complaisance.

Intent on his purpose, however, he inhaled and spoke again. ''At the Cantywell ball, I learned that my cousin meant to meet your sister in the library. I had no doubt the two of them would kick up a scandal if they were left to their own devices, and so I insisted that Marcheek tell Miss Vickery at the outset that he did not intend marriage. He protested, giving a hundred reasons why he felt obliged to refuse, not the least of which was that he was too pigeon-hearted to tell a female the truth.

The upshot was that we exchanged coats and masks and I went to the library in his place. All would have gone off smoothly if you had not come in. I expect you recall what happened then.''

"You kissed me.''

He looked away. After a pause, he went on. "Because the events in the library did not put an end to the flirtation between Marcheek and Miss Vickery, I felt obliged to continue to meet you. At least, that is the excuse I gave myself. It was not long before I became aware of my singular attachment to you. As soon as I did, I wished to reveal my true identity but was always prevented for one reason or another. Disclosing the truth was made peculiarly difficult by a fact brought home to me on more than one occasion—namely, that you despised James Bradford and could only love the man in the mask of white satin. I wished to be that man for as long as I possibly could. In that, I was remiss, perhaps, but though I can—and do—apologize, I cannot say that I regret it.''

This speech pleased her greatly. His face, so fully exposed to view that one or two stray droplets of rain shone on it, revealed to her how genuine his words were. Though he appeared tranquil as ever and spoke with the ease which she had earlier mistaken for sarcasm, his feelings were visible.

"Mr. Bradford,'' she said in a measured voice,

"I thank you for the trouble you have taken to relate these facts to me."

"Well, then, I suppose there is nothing further to say. I could not leave England without telling you everything myself, even though you already knew it. Honour demanded that you hear the truth from my own lips. And so, good night, Cassandra. Accept, if you will, my best wishes." He replaced his hat and walked to the steps.

She stopped him with "As I may never see you again, I should like to take this opportunity to thank you for your efforts on behalf of my sister. If Julia is well and safely married, it is due, in part, to you."

He acknowledged her thanks with a nod, then moved to go.

She called out, "I thank you also for devising the journey to London, which I must always look upon as the greatest adventure of my life."

With one foot on the step, the other on the floor of the temple, he faced her and regarded her with curiosity.

She saw that he was as pleasing to look at now as when he appeared masked. "Finally," she said, "I thank you for going against my wishes and bringing my pictures to Mr. Fuseli."

He said nothing, but she could see that he was affected.

"And now, having thanked you," she said, "I must beg a favour."

"If it is the favour of my absence, you need not put yourself to the trouble. You made it perfectly plain at our last meeting that the sight of James Bradford is hateful to your eyes. Rest assured, I intend to take my leave at once."

"That was not precisely what I had in view." She drew near.

"Perhaps you wish to have a green silk bonnet?"

She smiled. "I believe I should prefer to have a wedding ring, that is, if you will be so kind as to renew your offer of marriage to me."

Cautiously, he came to her. Because the mask was in his hand and not on his face, she could read his disbelief clearly.

"Why do you wish to marry me?" he asked. "After all, you are safe from Ned Bumpers now."

Blushing, she said, "I do not quite know how to explain my reasons. I fear it would take a very long time, and you appear to be in a great hurry."

"I do not leave Cantywell until daylight. That gives you six hours or thereabouts."

She looked about her. "But the rain is beginning to fall heavily."

"We shall be reasonably dry in the temple."

"You must give me a moment to think." On that, she put her hand to her brow and assumed an attitude of deep contemplation. At last, she declared, "I think I have it. The explanation is this." Here she put her hand to his cheek and kissed him. He scarcely returned the kiss at first, so that she drew a little away to search his eyes. She could see that he was not yet sure of her and was unwilling, therefore, to completely let down his guard.

"I see I have not made myself fully understood," she said, and kissed him again, with such sweetness this time that he could not keep his feelings in check for long. He held her ardently and more than returned her kiss. Cassandra felt that even Marietta, for all her flying about the ocean waves and hopping from flower to flower, had never experienced such happiness.

At the first opportunity, Mr. Bradford said, "You are no longer angry with me, I collect."

"I am no longer angry, but you must confess, you were very wicked."

"As were you."

"I was not wicked. I was merely curious."

"I see. Well, I suppose I shall have to marry you, so that we may put an end to all curiosity and make you respectable and dull, like other folks."

"After the past weeks, respectability and dullness will prove a novelty."

"Shall you like to honeymoon in China?"

"Yes, if you will promise me that on our return,

we shall go to Vauxhall. I should like to visit it as myself instead of as Mademoiselle de la Bellebonnette, and I should like to visit in the company of Mr. Bradford instead of Lord Marcheek.''

He gave his promise in the form of a kiss.

''And promise,'' she said when her lips were at liberty, ''that you will not lie to me ever again. A lady may like a masquerade now and again while she is being courted, but after marriage, she likes to know precisely who it is she is kissing.''

Again, his pledge was delivered in the form of a kiss, and one so lingering that they did not hear Mrs. Clapshew approach, saying as she came, ''I vow, we shall all catch our death in this downpour. I said to him, 'Sir, if we do not meet up with a rainstorm tonight, then I much mistake myself,' but would he heed me? Not by a long chalk. And this is the result: I am soaked to my skin and the two of you are—'' And here she was struck dumb at the sight of the lovers kissing. The mask of white satin had fallen to the floor.

Though she waited for what seemed to her a shocking length of time, the lovers did not desist. Thus, she cleared her throat, giving a credible imitation of a thunderclap.

Cassandra and Mr. Bradford turned to her, smiling.

''It is all right, Mrs. Clapshew,'' Cassandra assured her, ''we are to be married.''

"I should hope so, with such carryings-on! But until you, miss, are a bride signed and sealed, you will need a chaperon, and as I am so unfortunate as to hold that office, I shall take you home this instant. If you have anything to say to that, sir, you may say it, but be warned, it shall do you no good."

He approached her. "There is no use in scowling at us, Mrs. Clapshew. You may as well admit it—you intended this marriage from the outset, just as I did, and are now as pleased with yourself as the cat who dined on canary." So saying, he planted a kiss on her brow.

Cassandra added warmly, "If it is true that you meant to forward a match between us, old friend, then I must thank you for your excellent success." She, too, kissed the housekeeper's forehead.

Blushing with pleasure, Mrs. Clapshew could scarcely speak. "Flummery," she contrived to reply at last, and lest they glimpse her fluster, she stooped and picked up the mask.

"With your permission, I shall take that," said Mr. Bradford, "in case my wife should ever wish to have me wear it."

Mrs. Clapshew clucked severely at this daring notion and handed it over, saying, "Take the mask with good riddance. But if you should ever have cause to put it to use again, sir, you will do me the honour of not mentioning it to me." Then, turning and jutting out her chin, she pointed her umbrella forward as though she meant to joust with the elements, and thus made her way into the rain.

Mr. Bradford took Cassandra's hand and put it to his lips. Then he folded it in his arm so that, together, they might follow in Mrs. Clapshew's wake, smiling with contentment, though they were muddied, windblown and soaked.

MILLS & BOON®

Makes any time special™

**Mills & Boon publish 29 new titles
every month. Select from...**

Modern Romance™   Tender Romance™

Sensual Romance™

Medical Romance™   Historical Romance™

MAT2